"We'll never know if you don't try, will we?"

"I'll tell you what," he said. "I'll make a deal with you."

"What kind of a deal?" Miriam's expression was cautious.

"I promise to do everything you say…to try my hardest…for a month. If I'm not much better by then, you agree to quit."

Miriam stood very still, considering before she spoke. "I can't speak for Tim. Just for myself."

"*Yah.* Just for yourself."

"Who's going to decide whether or not you're much better?" she said. "You?"

His jaw hardened. She wasn't going to make this easy.

"No," he said abruptly. "How about…Betsy?"

Her lips twitched. "Don't you think Betsy has her own reasons for wanting to be rid of me?"

He raised one eyebrow, a gesture that used to work with the girls. "If you're really making progress, you'll have won her over by then. What's wrong? Don't you have any confidence in your work?"

She seemed to wince at that. After a long moment, she nodded. "All right. It's a deal."

A lifetime spent in rural Pennsylvania and her Pennsylvania Dutch heritage led **Marta Perry** to write about the Plain people, who add so much richness to her home state. Marta has seen over seventy of her books published, with over seven million books in print. She and her husband live in a beautiful central-Pennsylvania valley noted for its farms and orchards. When she's not writing, she's reading, traveling, baking or enjoying her six beautiful grandchildren.

Books by Marta Perry

Brides of Lost Creek

Second Chance Amish Bride
The Wedding Quilt Bride
The Promised Amish Bride
The Amish Widow's Heart
A Secret Amish Crush
Nursing Her Amish Neighbor

An Amish Family Christmas
"Heart of Christmas"
Amish Christmas Blessings
"The Midwife's Christmas Surprise"

Visit the Author Profile page at LoveInspired.com for more titles.

Nursing Her Amish Neighbor

Marta Perry

LOVE INSPIRED
INSPIRATIONAL ROMANCE

LOVE INSPIRED®
INSPIRATIONAL ROMANCE

Recycling programs
for this product may
not exist in your area.

ISBN-13: 978-1-335-75897-2

Nursing Her Amish Neighbor

This edition published by arrangement with Harlequin Books S.A.

For questions and comments about the quality of this book, please contact us at CustomerService@Harlequin.com.

Love Inspired
22 Adelaide St. West, 40th Floor
Toronto, Ontario M5H 4E3, Canada
www.LoveInspired.com

Printed in U.S.A.

For if ye forgive men their trespasses,
your heavenly Father will also forgive you.
—*Matthew* 6:14

This story is dedicated to all those
who work toward healing in the world.
And, as always, to my husband.

Chapter One

Matthew King heard the footsteps on the back porch and knew his father had finally come home. He'd been over at the Stoltzfus place next door long enough... talking about Matt, he felt sure. It was dark already, although the daylight lingered long on these August evenings.

Daad would come into the old farmhouse quietly, not wanting to wake the household, and especially Matt, sleeping on the first floor since the accident.

But Matt wasn't asleep. He didn't sleep much anymore, not unless he took those little white pills that the doctor had prescribed. And he didn't even have them at hand. Daad had insisted they be kept in one of the kitchen cabinets, maybe afraid of what Matt might do if they were too easily accessible.

However appealing oblivion might be, even on the worst days, he'd never take that way out. It would be too hard on his parents, as well as being a violation of their faith. He wasn't sure he even cared about that any longer, but they did.

Matt shoved the pillow up behind him, his gaze wandering around the room. They'd put him in the sewing room, so he could be on the ground floor. The quilting frame was still propped against the wall, and the sewing machine, covered with a sheet, sat in the corner. Inconveniencing everyone, that was what he was doing. Better if he had died in the accident, like David.

The familiar pain and grief swamped him, only to be chased away by rage. Better if he had died *instead* of David, that was what he thought. And certain sure better if that reckless drunken teenager had killed himself instead of David. But no, he'd walked away with hardly a scratch, while Matt's family's lives were changed forever.

Forgive, said the church. But this wasn't something he could forgive. The bishop came to see him, praying for him, sitting endlessly beside the bed. *Time*, he'd said. *Give it time. God's purposes will become clear. Our job is just to obey.*

But all the time in the world wouldn't make this any better. David was gone.

The back door closed softly, and he heard Daad's quiet footsteps cross the wide boards of the kitchen floor and stop. He must have walked to the hall and waited, looking and listening. He'd see that the light was still lit in Matt's room. He'd come in.

Sure enough, the footsteps approached. A slight tap on the door was followed by the door opening, and Daad stepped inside.

"Everyone else asleep?" he asked.

Matt shrugged. "They went up a half hour ago. Whether they're sleeping, I couldn't say. Well, did you convince Miriam to take on the hopeless case?"

He could hear the bitterness in his voice. He wanted to take it away, but he couldn't.

Daad's weathered face tightened. "It is not hopeless. Nothing in God's creation is hopeless unless people make it so. And yah, Miriam has agreed to come and help us."

"Maybe she can help Mamm. She can't help me." His jaw set. "And she won't be around very long."

He'd make sure of that.

Daad's lips quirked in what might have been a smile. "Wait and see. You may be surprised."

Matt shook this off impatiently. "That little thing? Shy and serious and afraid of her own shadow? She's not going to make any difference to me."

He was being unfair to Miriam, he knew. And Daad knew it, too. That's why he was frowning, but he didn't say anything more about Miriam. Instead he glanced around the room.

"Do you need anything before I go up?"

Just a new pair of legs, he thought, the bitterness engulfing him. But he wouldn't say it. Daad had enough to bear without him pitying himself.

He shook his head. "Good night, Daad."

"Good night, son." His father went out quickly, probably glad to leave the sound and smell of the sickroom behind.

Matt shoved at the pillow again. Daad might be confident about Miriam, but he figured he knew her better after growing up next door. She was a sweet kid, but there was no way she'd get him to do anything he didn't want to do. And he didn't want to waste his time on exercises that wouldn't make him the man he'd been before.

No, Miriam could try her best. But he was a hopeless case, and the sooner she accepted that, the better it would be for both of them.

Miriam Stoltzfus walked along the edge of the pasture that stretched between her parents' farm and that of the King family, trying not to think about what she'd gotten herself into. The August sun beat down, hot already though it wasn't noon yet, increasing her discomfort.

Most of that discomfort came not from the temperature, but from her own feelings about accepting this new challenge. After all, she'd just returned from a lengthy stay with relatives out in Ohio, helping with a new baby, then with her aunt's recovery from surgery, and then…

She'd as soon forget what had happened next.

In recent years, word had gotten around in the close-knit Amish communities that Miriam Stoltzfus, still unmarried at twenty-six, had a gift for helping out when folks were sick or injured, and the requests had been thick and fast in the past year. She'd come home hoping for a rest, only to be confronted by Abel King, who was distraught over the loss of one son and desperately worried about the recovery of the other.

The two families had been neighbors for generations. It wasn't possible to turn down a request like that. So here she was, approaching the King farmhouse, more than apprehensive about what she was going to find. Her own confidence was at an all-time low, and Matthew King had certain sure never lacked for that quality. If he didn't want her here—

With a silent prayer for help, she paused at the screen door.

She hadn't timed that very well, since their family was obviously getting lunch on the table. But Abel spotted her and waved her in.

"Wilkom, Miriam. Will you join us for a bite?"

Elizabeth glanced up from the stove at the sound of her husband's voice. She didn't speak, but Miriam was shocked at the sight of her. Elizabeth's worn, pale face seemed to have been wiped free of all emotion. She moved mechanically, ladling chicken potpie into a bowl for serving. It was if she'd turned her inner self off, leaving only the outer shell.

Miriam collected herself with an effort. "No, denke." She tried to smile at Abel, tried to sound normal. "I ate before I left home. Don't let me interrupt you. Can I help?"

She glanced around the kitchen, in some ways a replica of theirs next door, with its wooden cabinets and long oak table, except that this table was oval instead of rectangular. And smaller. The King family had been much smaller than theirs, with Matt, David and Betsy the only children. Betsy stood at the counter near the stove, putting dishes on a tray—for Matt, obviously.

As if feeling her gaze, fourteen-year-old Betsy looked up and murmured a welcome, but the wariness in her blue eyes seemed to deny the words.

Curious at her reaction, Miriam crossed the kitchen to her. Betsy had buttered two slices of bread and cut them into small pieces, and now she was cutting up the morsels of noodles and chicken in the potpie.

Odd. From what she'd been told, she'd thought Matt's injuries were mostly to his legs.

Trying to be helpful, she reached for the tray. "Why don't you go ahead and eat, Betsy? I'll take this—"

"No!" Betsy grabbed the tray and jerked it away from her. "I'll take Matt's meal. I always do." The accompanying glare suggested Miriam had better back off.

"If you want," she said, keeping her voice mild, but she didn't back away. She wasn't going to be intimidated by a teenager. "But I did come to help with Matt, after all."

Betsy's eyes widened. She spun, zeroing in on her father with a look of outrage. "You didn't say anything to me about this." Her voice rose. "I can take care of Matt perfectly well. I don't need anybody's help."

So Abel hadn't told anyone about his plans—or at least, not Betsy.

A glance at Elizabeth didn't make things any clearer. Either she hadn't known, or if he'd spoken, the words hadn't registered with her, caught as she was in her frozen state.

But Betsy was the immediate problem, not her mother.

"That's enough, Betsy." Abel sounded weary. "We need more help. You shouldn't spend all your time with Matthew. Your mother needs your help with the house and garden."

"Matt's recovery is more important!" she flared.

"Yah, it is." His voice had hardened. "Miriam has had experience in taking care of injured people, and she knows how to work with the therapist."

"Matt doesn't want—"

"Enough," he repeated. He didn't raise his voice, but there was no doubt that he'd meant it. After a moment's hesitation, Betsy turned away, silenced.

Abel's reaction might not have helped Miriam in Betsy's eyes, but maybe nothing would have. Betsy clearly considered Matt's well-being her responsibility.

As for Elizabeth, she didn't even seem to have noticed that anything had happened. She just moved from the stove to the table like some sort of machine, and Miriam watched her with shocked pity.

She'd told herself that her only job here was to help Matt, but it seemed clear now that she wouldn't be able to do that without becoming involved with the rest of the family. Her heart sank at the enormity of the task.

Betsy, seeming to sense victory about lunch, at least, picked up the tray defiantly and started down the hall. Miriam moved just as quickly, right behind her. When the girl turned to glare, she just smiled.

"I'll hold the door for you." Before Betsy could react, she moved past the pantry and opened the door leading to what had been Elizabeth's quilting room. It was the only space downstairs that could have been turned into a room for Matthew.

Betsy gritted her teeth, but she gave a short nod and passed into the room. She reached for the door, obviously intending to shut Miriam out, but Miriam slipped inside and closed the door, never letting go of her smile.

Matthew sat on the bed, propped against pillows. He'd clearly been expecting only his sister, because after one shocked look at Miriam, he turned his head away quickly.

Not quite fast enough, though. The right side of his face, with his even features, strong jaw and well-shaped mouth, looked much as usual, except for the pallor and strain that was evident. But the left side—

Her breath caught. A jagged scar ran down his face from the outer corner of his eye to his mouth, twisting it out of resemblance to the right. Her heart winced at the pain he'd been through.

Betsy hesitated a moment, as if waiting for an outburst, and then scurried over to him, setting the tray on a bedside table. "Your favorite thing today—chicken potpie. I've cut it up to make it easier for you to eat."

He grunted, and she seemed to take that for agreement. Betsy began spreading a napkin over his chest, as if he were a messy toddler.

Not wanting to precipitate another outburst from Betsy, Miriam looked around the room while observing them in brief glances. Matt was ignoring her, although he certainly knew why she was here.

That was all right. She intended to watch this time, see what the situation was, and talk to the therapist.

That would give Miriam enough to think about for her first visit.

When the room had been Elizabeth's quilting room, it was constantly in use. Elizabeth's beautifully designed, colorful quilts had been very popular at craft fairs and auctions, and her family had beamed with pride when one fetched the highest price at last year's spring auction.

But now the quilting frame was shoved against the wall, actually gathering dust, something that was ordinarily unheard-of in Elizabeth's spotless house. A basket and several blankets were piled atop the treadle sewing machine in the corner, making it clear that it was unused, as well.

It wasn't a bad room for someone recovering— bigger than most bedrooms, with two windows on the side and one looking out the back, so that Matt would have views both of the meadow between their two farms and the normally busy farmyard and barn behind the house.

He didn't act as if he enjoyed the views, though. He stared at the walls even while his sister fussed over him, holding the bowl at what seemed to Miriam an awkward height.

Did Matt really need someone to help him eat? He didn't seem to, but he submitted tamely to Betsy's fussing, darting a glance toward Miriam once or twice, as if to be sure she saw that he didn't need her help.

Finally he pushed Betsy's hands away with an annoyed movement. "That's enough," he muttered.

"Come on," she coaxed. "Just a few more bites,

please? You can do it." She spoke as if he were a two-year-old.

Had he been putting up with that? He must have been, she supposed. But something, maybe Miriam's presence, made him object today.

"I said it was enough. Take it away and stop fussing."

Looking hurt, Betsy collected the tray. Once again, Miriam held the door. Then she closed it behind Betsy and turned to him, steeling herself for trouble.

"Well? Tell me you're not shocked at the change in me." His tone was edged, taunting her to say no.

"Just a bit," she said mildly. "I guess you have changed. You didn't used to expect people to wait on you."

It took him a couple of seconds to get what she was saying, and then his face darkened with anger.

But before he could speak, the door opened again, revealing Abel, gesturing to her. The argument Matt clearly wanted to have would have to wait. Well, thinking out what he wanted to say would at least keep him from staring at the walls.

She couldn't count on help from Matt's mother or sister, it seemed, but she wouldn't give up. Matt had her to deal with now, and she'd push him for his own good. She stepped into the hall. An Englischer stood waiting behind Abel, watching her with a twinkle in his brown eyes—undoubtedly the physical therapist.

Matt glared at the door, feeling as if his thoughts ought to burn right through it. Nothing happened to the door, and he resisted the impulse to throw something at it, just to make clear how he felt.

When his ire lessened enough so that he could concentrate on something else, he realized he could hear the murmur of voices from the hallway. Miriam's was one, that was certain sure, and after a moment, he recognized the other as that of Tim, the therapist.

He gritted his teeth. He should have known Miriam would be expecting to talk to the therapist. Probably Daad had set it up that way. He hated the idea of anyone discussing him, especially those two.

And he also didn't like what Miriam had implied with her smart comment. Apparently she wasn't as quiet and shy as he'd always thought, to talk back to him that way.

What had she meant, anyway? Did she think he was making too much of his physical problems? Or that he was pitying himself?

No, he didn't need Betsy's fussing over him, but it wasn't Miriam's business. Besides, it seemed to make Betsy happy to do something for him.

He'd gotten that far in his figuring when someone tapped on the door and opened it.

"Hey, Matt, are you ready for me?" Tim Considine didn't wait for an answer, just came in with his usual good cheer.

"Ready as I'll be..." Matt stopped, frowning, as Miriam slipped in behind him. "What's Miriam doing here? I don't need an audience when you're working on my legs."

Tim quirked an eyebrow as he shook his head.

"Come on, now. Miriam has signed on to help with your daily workout. She has to see how I want it done." Tim grinned. "No need to worry about her. She's done this before, right, Miriam?"

"That's right." Miriam's pleasant face might have shown a little wariness now. Maybe she knew he had an outburst waiting for when they were alone. And maybe that wariness meant a little pushing would convince her this wasn't going to work.

"I'm not worried. And I don't need anyone to help me."

"Can't fool me." Tim shoved back the sheet, his hands moving deftly along Matt's legs. "You haven't done a single exercise since last week, have you?"

Matt set his jaw. Just about anything he said would be a lie. He had endured the exercises Tim pushed him through, but he certain sure wasn't willing to do any extra ones.

"Right." Tim read the answer in his face. "This time you'll have someone to help you through them."

An objection came to his lips, but Tim shook his head. "Your father says you agreed to this. Isn't that right?"

He didn't have an answer to this one, either. Maybe he'd have to put up with Miriam for a few days. But with a little effort, he ought to be able to make the experience unpleasant enough that she'd quit herself.

Contenting himself with that, Matt nodded.

"Okay, let's get busy." Tim rubbed his hands together. "Come over here where you can see what's going on, Miriam."

As she moved closer, Tim started in on his routine. This time he explained what was happening while he went, showing Miriam exactly what was wrong and how to work the muscles. Matt discovered he was listening just as Miriam was, understanding a little better what was happening with his useless legs.

"You want to push to the point of resistance, ease up and then repeat. Let's try four or five repetitions of each exercise this week." His easy grin came again as Miriam scribbled notes on a pad. "Not so little that he doesn't have to work, but not so much that he tries to throw something at you."

Miriam's answering smile suggested that she knew Matt wanted to do just that. "I'll duck if I have to."

"Right. Now just put your hands where I had mine, and you can try it."

Before Matt could protest, Miriam's hands had replaced Tim's, grasping his leg firmly but gently. Hers were smaller than Tim's, but he was more aware of them. He could feel their warmth through the loose pants he wore.

He had to admit she seemed capable enough, and she moved his leg exactly as Tim had done.

"How's that? A little farther?" She studied his face as if she'd read the answer there.

Gritting his teeth, he nodded. His muscles screamed in protest, but he sure wasn't going to let Miriam know it.

Tim moved on through the exercises, showing, teaching and then watching as Miriam did the same. Only once or twice did he have to stop her and correct something. Matt found himself annoyed by Miriam's ability. He didn't want her working on him. He didn't want anybody doing it. Why couldn't they just leave him alone? He was useless no matter what they did.

As for Miriam…well, he suspected she had to know when she pushed his leg to the point of pain, but she wouldn't let it show in her face, any more than he would. They had that in common, at least.

"You can feel how strong his leg muscles are, even now," Tim was telling her. "But it's important that we work on the arm strength, as well. We don't want him to lose muscle mass because of lack of use."

Miriam nodded. "It's encouraging that he's so strong to begin with, ain't so?" She didn't glance at him, but Matt thought a faint flush of color moved through her cheeks.

"Yes," Tim said. He patted Matt's arm in a friendly way. "Gives you a much better chance of getting off this bed and busy again."

A spark of anger flickered in Matt. "Will it get me back in the fields again, where I need to be? Because if not, it doesn't matter to me."

Tim drew back, startled by the bitterness in his voice, and Matt regretted losing control. It wasn't Tim's fault, but…

"It matters to other folk." Miriam's voice didn't lose its gentleness, but there was a thread of disapproval he could certain sure hear. "Like your parents, and your sister, and a bunch of other people who care about you."

"All right," he growled, knowing the rebuke was

justified, but he was annoyed all the same. "Are you about finished?"

"Just the massage left." Tim glanced at Matt's legs and hesitated.

Matt figured he knew what was in his mind. Last week Tim had helped him remove the pants for the massage. Well, he certain sure wasn't going to have Miriam doing that. And it looked as if Tim had figured that out for himself.

"Maybe your father could help with this," Tim began, sounding doubtful. He must know how busy Daad was with no one to help him on the farm.

"That won't work." He'd sooner do without the massage than add something else to Daad's workload.

"Suppose we spread the sheet over his legs and do it that way," Miriam suggested. "It will work better than nothing."

"Not a bad idea. Let's give it a try." Between them, they spread out the sheet. "You've done massage this way before?"

"Yah. The last…" Her voice faded, and she took a breath. "The last young man I helped had badly swollen, painful joints, and the massage eased his pain."

Tim nodded, and they went off onto a technical discussion of what had been wrong with that person, probably someone she'd helped while she was out in Ohio. Matt didn't bother listening, because he was too busy wondering what had caused that sad expression on Miriam's face.

Who was he? And why did the mention of him bring

that mingling of pain and embarrassment to Miriam's face? If he wanted a way to get rid of her, it might be worthwhile for him to find out.

Chapter Two

Miriam had avoided the angry encounter Matthew had undoubtedly looked forward to by the simple method of walking out with the therapist. After consulting with him and assuring Abel that she'd be back in midmorning to do the first of two workouts each day that Tim recommended, she'd headed for home. She'd been shaken enough by seeing what had become of the Matthew she'd known. She hadn't needed to stick around and be a target for his obvious displeasure.

The lively conversation around the supper table kept her thoughts occupied—with her six younger brothers, there was never any lack of chatter, even though Aaron was married now and had his own small house on the property. That still left five others ranging from eight to twenty to keep up the noise level.

No, she certain sure wouldn't talk about Matthew over supper. She'd wait until she could be alone with Mammi.

Eventually the kitchen cleared out, since there were

evening chores to be done. Miriam and Mammi automatically began to tackle the dishes. After the final banging of the back door, her mother gave her a questioning look.

"Are you going over to see Matthew tomorrow?" A slight shadow of doubt crossed her face as she said the words.

"Not until midmorning." She raised her voice above the rush of hot water into the sink. "Tim, the physical therapist, wants me to do two workouts a day—one in midmorning, one in midafternoon. I'll try to do whatever I can to help with him in between."

"I hope…" Mammi paused, and Miriam saw the doubt in her eyes. "I hope it works out."

"What is it, Mammi?" She reached over to clasp her mother's hand with her soapy one. "You're worried about this, ain't so?"

Mammi squeezed her hand. "Ach, I'm being foolish. But after the bad time you had, I was looking forward to having my daughter here so I could just baby you. You need a rest from taking care of people. I thought we could pick out material for a new dress, and can corn relish, and…"

Miriam didn't know whether to laugh or cry. Her mother had been thinking the same way she had…that those sweet, ordinary things of life would feel wonderful good after the trials she'd experienced lately.

"We will, Mammi. I promise you. Whether I end up being able to help Matthew or not, we'll make time for us to do things together."

"Good." Mammi wiped away a tear. "I can't very well take any of your bruders shopping with me, ain't so?"

The thought made Miriam chuckle, but that fact was a bit sorrowful, too. Mammi had really wanted another girl or two, Miriam knew, but she'd ended up with six boys. Boys, she always claimed, weren't quite as satisfactory in producing grandbabies for her. Not that Miriam had many hopes of doing that either at this point. Still, Aaron's wife, Anna Grace, had a good chance at it.

"Mammi, I know you've been over at the King place often enough to get an idea of how things are going. Do you think I'll be able to do anything with Matthew?"

Mammi wiped a bowl slowly, her face thoughtful.

"I'm not sure what's happening with Matthew since the accident, and I don't know that anyone else does. I guess it's natural that someone who's always taken his strength and good health for granted would be shaken by losing it all at once, but he's not even trying. He ought to see what it's doing to his father, it seems to me."

Even that mild a criticism was rare from Mammi, who always saw the best in everyone. It sounded as if Matt's whole personality had changed.

Well, she'd seen that for herself. "Maybe he needs a little more time," she suggested. "He's grieving for his brother, too. Maybe even feels responsible since he was driving, though how he could have avoided that drunk driver, I don't know. Still, I have the physical therapist on my side, at least. We'll gang up on him if we have to," she added lightly.

Her mother managed a smile, but Miriam could see that she was still worried.

"I just don't want you to be hurt. If you don't get anywhere with Matthew, it won't be your fault, any more than what happened with your aunt's neighbor was."

Miriam winced at the reference to her painful experience in Ohio. Poor Wayne. She couldn't help but wonder how he was faring, despite being told in no uncertain terms to stay away from him.

"I can't do more than try," she said, wishing she could chase away her mother's worry, to say nothing of her own. "You know what Daad always taught us kids. That if we failed at something, we just had to try again."

"Some things it's better not to try again. Like the time Sammy climbed up to the barn roof," Mamm said. "Your daad certain sure didn't want him to try that again. Some things are best not repeated."

"I remember, only too well. I'm the one who had to go up and talk him down." She grinned, remembering the expression red-haired Sammy wore when she'd finally eased him back down to the ground. He'd been proud as could be, right up to the moment when Daad had taken the switch to him for being so foolish.

"Sammy hasn't changed, for all that he's ten now," Mamm said, trying to suppress a smile. "Your daad caught him trying to ride that old mule the other day."

"What happened?" She remembered the mule—the worst-tempered creature that God had ever created, Daad always said.

"It ran him right into the barn wall and then kicked him for good measure. Your daad thinks that might teach him a lesson, but I don't believe anything ever will." Mamm looked exasperated.

"He's still trying to find something his big brothers haven't done, I guess. That's what it is to have older siblings."

That made her think of Betsy, the baby of the King family. Surely it would be possible to get Betsy to see that babying Matthew wasn't helping him.

But her job would be Matthew, not Betsy. Nor their mother, who was so lost in her grief.

"About Elizabeth…" she began tentatively.

Mammi shook her head. "I've tried to get her to talk about it, but she just can't. You know how she always doted on David. You'd think it would have been Betsy, the youngest, who was the one she'd spoiled, but it was always David."

Miriam remembered. "I don't believe it was possible for anyone to spoil David. He had such a sweet nature."

"No, it didn't spoil David," Mammi agreed. She frowned, as if groping for an answer to a riddle. "But I was thinking more about Betsy. This has been hard on her. She's the only one of the kinder who was untouched by the accident."

Miriam found herself shaking her head. No, surely Betsy hadn't been untouched by the accident. It had turned her whole family upside down and would have affected her in ways she might not even recognize. Maybe…

She reminded herself again that Betsy wasn't her

job. But she had a feeling that between them, both of the remaining King siblings were going to try her fragile confidence to the breaking point.

Miriam hurried along the edge of the pasture toward the King place the next morning. She'd have to pick up her pace to be on time, but she'd valued an early morning conversation with her mother too much to rush it. Mammi understood people, and she'd known Elizabeth and Abel all her married life. Maybe, with both of them thinking about it, they'd see some way to help them. As for Matthew, it seemed he was going to be her responsibility.

With her forehead furrowed in thoughts of Matt, her brother Joshua, coming toward her, had almost reached her before she realized he was there.

"Finished helping Abel already?" She knew he'd headed out before dawn to help Matt's father get crates of vegetables hauled to the co-op for the produce auction.

Joshua stopped, smiling down at her—he'd been enjoying looking down at his big sister ever since he'd passed her in height. At seventeen, he probably wasn't finished growing yet, either. And she still had to go through it with Sammy and the twins.

"Yah, we're done for now. I said I'd come back later to help Abel with the fencing."

"Maybe I'll see you there later, yah?" As she took a step, Joshua put out a hand to stop her.

"Can you wait a minute? I want to ask you something."

As far as she could tell, Matt wouldn't care if she ever got there, so she decided to stop worrying about it. "For sure. What is it?"

She studied Josh's face, noticing the maturity that had become more evident in the months she'd been away. As the middle of seven children, he'd always been quieter than easygoing, popular Daniel, three years older, and Sammy, almost seven years younger, the energetic schnickelfritz who was always into everything. He wasn't one to whip out an answer. If you wanted to know what was on Josh's mind, you had to wait patiently.

"It's Abel," he said finally. "He wants me to come work for him—like a regular job, I mean, not just helping out."

He stopped there. It seemed something about the offer bothered him, but she wasn't sure what.

"If you don't like that sort of work…" she began, but he shook his head vigorously.

"It's not that. I like it. Even better than dairying." He darted an apprehensive look around, as if afraid Daad would hear him. Their branch of the Stoltzfus family had been dairy farmers for three generations.

She waited. There was more, or else Joshua wouldn't wear that line between his brows.

"Abel wants to pay me," he said, all in one breath. "I don't know…well, we're neighbors. I'd help him anyway. It feels funny him wanting to pay me for it."

Probably only Joshua, with his sensitive conscience, would worry about such a thing. She squeezed his hand. "I think it's all right. Naturally he'd pay anyone else he hired. If you want to do it, it seems like a gut job for you."

When he looked unconvinced, she added, "Talk to Daad about it. He'll know the right thing to do, ain't so?"

"Yah, that's true." A smile wiped away the line. "Denke, Miriam." He squeezed her hand in return, his blue eyes cleared of worry, and then trotted off toward home, his burden lifted.

It was a small thing, she knew, but Miriam felt satisfied in a way she hadn't in quite a while. She shouldn't have stayed away so long, letting her little brothers grow up without her. They counted on her. This was where she belonged…in this valley, with the people who knew her and cared for her.

Reminding herself that she had someone to help today, she hurried on across the field.

Miriam's muscles tightened as she thought ahead to what awaited her. Matthew had been annoyed with her the day before, and he hadn't had an opportunity to vent that annoyance. The Matt she'd known and grown up with had never held on to a grudge overnight, but Matt as he was since the accident…well, she couldn't be sure of his reaction. And if there was one thing she disliked, it was confronting someone.

To her surprise, Elizabeth was out in the garden, and even more surprising, Betsy was with her. Apparently Abel's words had borne some fruit. If Betsy could get her mother to take an interest in things, that would help both of them.

Waving to them, she hurried inside, reaching the

door to Matt's room slightly out of breath. She paused for a moment, collecting herself, tapped lightly, and opened the door.

"You're late." Matt shoved himself up onto his elbows to level the words at her, and Miriam had to smile. If annoyance with her produced that much energy, maybe she should annoy him every day.

"Yah, I am, a little. Sorry. I met Joshua coming over."

That distracted him, as she'd hoped, giving her a moment to assess his condition today. He seemed to have a bit more color and life in his face, maybe the effect of having something to complain about.

"Joshua told you about Daad's offer, ain't so?" He sank back on his pillow.

"Do you mind?" She moved a little closer. She'd learned to read feelings on people's faces since she'd been home nursing, but Matt managed to evade her with his closed expression.

His hands clenched into fists. "If I weren't stuck in this bed, Daad wouldn't have to be hiring anyone to help him."

There was the crux of the matter, and Miriam knew she'd have to meet it head-on if she were to help him.

"No, I guess not. If the accident hadn't happened, a lot of things would be different." She grasped his right leg, wondering how much he'd cooperate without Tim standing beside her.

He jumped in response, but then he seemed to force himself not to react. His eyes narrowed.

"Aren't you going to accuse me of self-pity? Or…

what was it you said yesterday? Of wanting people to fuss over me?"

Miriam forced herself to adopt the calm mannerism that she used with complaining patients. "I suspected you wanted to yell at me over that. Go ahead, if you want."

That seemed to disarm him, and he gave her a reluctant smile. It changed quickly to a wince as she lifted his leg.

Noting it, she regretted she hadn't warned him before the movement. "Let's start with some leg stretches, yah?"

"Seems like you already started." He was gritting his teeth. "I was going to say it's no fun yelling at someone when they've given you permission."

Miriam was cheered by the trace of humor in his voice. That was more like the Matt she remembered. "That's why I did it," she said lightly. "You know, you can tell me to ease off whenever you think I'm going too far," she reminded him.

"Would you listen?" he retorted. "Never mind, don't answer that."

"We do want to increase the angle of lift before Tim comes back, ain't so?" She eased the right leg down and moved around to the left. She'd come back to it for more exercise once he was warmed up.

He didn't answer, and she gave him a questioning look. He was eyeing her. "You'd like to please Tim, yah? He's a good-looking guy."

What was on his mind now? Did he intend to tease

her about the physical therapist? If so, he was really on the wrong track.

"You're the one who's supposed to please him." His earlier comment about his father having to pay someone to help out came back to her. That might be a way to get him motivated. "You don't want your daad to have to pay for extra therapy sessions, do you?"

"I don't want him paying for any," he snapped, his fragmentary good humor gone. "You don't need to remind me of what I'm costing my family. But if I can't be the way I was, what use is it?"

Well, she'd wanted him to be motivated, but that was the wrong reaction. "If you can't do what you did, you might find you can be useful in another way," she said. She watched his face to see how he took that idea, but once again, he'd frozen her out.

Well, she'd come back to it. "Let's push you up on the pillow a bit before we do the bent leg stretches. Okay?"

Taking his silence for assent she bent to help lift him at the same moment he reared up on his elbows. Their foreheads cracked together, and she closed her eyes. When she opened them, his face was inches away... close enough to see every tiny line, to feel his every breath.

Her own breath caught in her throat, and she forced herself to push away from him. "Sorry." She managed a shaky smile. "I didn't mean to knock you out."

Matt didn't speak, and his face was unreadable. But if he really thought she was attracted to Tim, he was on the wrong track.

Wait a minute, she warned herself. She wasn't attracted to anyone. It was completely unsuitable to feel anything for either of them.

Matt rubbed his forehead, trying to get his mind straight. He hadn't expected that…well, that closeness with Miriam, even if it was accidental. She was looking at him, a bit anxious, and he had to say something.

"Tim never cracked his head on mine," he muttered.

"Well, you probably never interfered with his moving you."

That was completely different, as far as he was concerned. Tim was a professional, and a man, and there wasn't any shame about letting him help.

"Just tell me what you want me to do, and I'll do it myself. It'll probably be safer."

Miriam's lips twitched. "Learning how to move patients is part of being able to help them. You don't need to be afraid I'll drop you. Or that I'll hurt myself."

Her talent for figuring him out was mistaken this time. Fear wasn't what bothered him. The truth was, he didn't want Miriam helping him move because that made him too aware of his own weakness. He didn't think he'd say that to her, though.

"I'd have said you were too shy to do any such thing. What happened to the quiet, soft-spoken Miriam I used to know?"

She had taken hold of his leg again, this time moving his bent knee toward his chest. Once that had been taken for granted. Now it hurt so much he clenched his teeth.

"Easy," she said, bringing his leg back a few inches. "You're trying too hard to do it yourself. Let me move your leg for you. We're just working on flexibility." She pressed it again, very gently. "As far as shyness is concerned…well, I figured out that if I was going to help people, I sometimes had to be firm, even if I didn't feel it."

He breathed a sigh of relief as she eased his leg down and then started on the other one. "So that's just a mask you wear, yah?"

Miriam smiled. "You sound pleased. Do you think that will make it easier for you to push me out?"

She understood too much, he decided.

"I wouldn't do that," he said, and then wondered if that sounded as phony to her as it did to him. "I agreed to let you work with me, didn't I?"

"Yah, you did."

It seemed to him that she didn't sound convinced. It was almost as if she knew perfectly well what he had planned. He didn't like it.

Before he could figure out whether or not to deny it, the door opened, and Betsy burst in. "What are you doing?" She glared at Miriam as if suspicious of her actions, making him remember Miriam's comment about him enjoying Betsy fussing over him.

"Exercising," he said shortly. "Maybe you should go help Mammi." Not that he thought Miriam was right, but still…

"I already did. And anyway, if I watch, I can help if Miriam can't be here sometime." The smile she gave Miriam didn't convince him, although it might have convinced someone else. Betsy was up to something. Or maybe she just didn't want anyone else taking over what she considered her job.

"That's a gut idea," Miriam chipped in unexpectedly. "We're just going to start on some exercises for arm strength. Did you notice the attachments Tim rigged up overhead?"

Betsy nodded, moving a bit closer, while Miriam groped over her head, standing on tiptoe to point out the handholds of a couple of sets of cords.

"Tim said he wants you to start working with these this week. Eventually you can use them to help you sit up and to get in and out of bed."

He wanted to say that he didn't consider that much of a prize for hard work, but decided it wasn't worth it, especially with Betsy standing right there.

Was that why Miriam had been so interested in involving Betsy in what she was doing? Did she think his little sister's presence would make him try harder?

Actually, he'd begun to count on Betsy's willingness to do whatever he wanted. He wanted her on his side, not Miriam's, even if she thought what Miriam was doing was for his own good.

"For now, let's just do a few strength exercises." Miriam put a handgrip in each of his hands. "Try pulling yourself forward and up, as if you're going to sit up in bed."

He nodded, his muscles tightening as he pulled. And pulled. "Wouldn't have thought it would be so hard," he gasped. What had happened to him while those doctors were operating on him and keeping him under all that medication?

"It takes time to come back from lying in bed," Miriam said, as if she knew his thoughts. "I've heard a therapist say a week of exercise for every day in bed." She'd moved closer, and as he tried again, she put her hand on the middle of his back, pressing.

He could feel how much easier that made it to pull up. And he could also feel the shape of her palm and the warmth of her skin through the thin cotton of his nightshirt. He looked at her, feeling that awareness move between them.

"Here, let me help." Betsy charged in, inserting herself between him and Miriam.

Jealous? He couldn't be sure.

"That's right." Miriam, unruffled, moved Betsy's hand slightly. "Good. Now don't push. Just use your hand for a little extra support. We want his muscles to work but not strain."

"Yah, I see. I can feel it." Betsy sounded pleased, her antagonism slipping away.

With the two of them behind him, he couldn't see either of their faces. But he didn't like the idea of them ganging up on him.

"Betsy, do we have any lemonade?"

"I don't think so. Do you want some? I can make it." All her eagerness to please him rushed back.

"We could all use some after we finish here, ain't so? Why don't you make a pitcher?"

"Right away." She hurried off.

"Don't worry about it." Miriam seemed amused. "She's still your willing servant."

"That wasn't the idea," he said stiffly, his temper flaring that she could read him so easily. "In case you haven't noticed, it makes her happy to do things for me."

"I noticed." She looped the handles back up over the bar and pulled down a pair of stretchy bands. "As long as she's helping you to get stronger, I don't object."

"Stronger." He almost spat out the word. "Stronger for what? None of this is going to do any good. It's useless. I can't be the person I was."

She seemed unaffected by his anger. "We'll never know that if you don't try, will we?"

He glared at her for a long moment as a thought formed in his mind. He turned it over, looking at it from all angles. Would it work?

"I'll tell you what," he said. "I'll make a deal with you."

"What kind of a deal?" Miriam's expression was cautious.

"I promise to do everything you say…to try my hardest…for a month. If I'm not much better by then, you agree to quit."

Miriam stood very still, considering before she spoke. "I can't speak for Tim. Just for myself."

"Yah. Just for yourself."

"Who's going to decide whether or not you're much better?" she said. "You?"

His jaw hardened. She wasn't going to make this easy.

"No," he said abruptly. "How about… Betsy?"

Her lips twitched. "Don't you think Betsy has her own reasons for wanting to be rid of me?"

He raised one eyebrow, a gesture that used to attract the girls. "If you're really making progress, you'll have won her over by then. What's wrong? Don't you have any confidence in your work?"

She seemed to wince at that. After a long moment, she nodded. "All right. It's a deal."

Chapter Three

Over the next couple of days, second thoughts came back to haunt Miriam. Had she backed herself into a corner by coming to that agreement with Matt? Still, what else could she have done when he challenged her?

The truth was, if her work didn't have any good results in a month's time, there was no sense in Abel continuing to pay her for coming.

The fact that Abel was paying did give her pause. In a sense, she worked for him, not Matt. Should she tell him what she'd done in agreeing to Matt's demand?

Neither she nor Matt had said they would keep the deal to themselves, but she couldn't help feeling that it had been a private agreement between two childhood friends. If it worked as she hoped, it would be well worth it. Abel would be too pleased to care how it had come about.

So far Matt had been fulfilling his promise, although it was early days yet. She couldn't complain that he wasn't trying. In fact, when she saw how hard he pushed, she wanted to tell him to ease off.

Today's morning session was going well, with Matt using the stretchy bands to build muscle strength back in both his arms and legs. He actually seemed interested in using the bands, maybe because it pitted him against himself. She'd always thought him competitive.

"Good work," she said, rolling them back when he'd finished. "If you keep that up, you might be able to move to the next tighter bands by Monday."

He shrugged, leaning back against the raised slant of the hospital bed. "Such excitement. Will they be a different color?"

"As a matter of fact, they will."

His question had been sarcastic, she supposed, but it made her think of something that might be more exciting. She glanced around the room, with its sewing and quilting equipment shoved back against the walls and covered with sheets, like so many mounds of snow.

This room didn't have much to express the personality of the person living in it. Or to make it more cheerful and welcoming. Why hadn't she seen that before?

The door opened, admitting Betsy with a tray. "Lunch is ready, Miriam. Mammi says to come."

Leaving Betsy to cope with getting Matt to eat as best she could, Miriam walked into the kitchen and took her place at the table.

Once the silent prayer before the meal had finished, Miriam continued to sit quietly, mentally rearranging furniture, until Abel put down his fork and looked at her.

"Was ist letz? Is something wrong, Miriam? You are not usually so quiet. And you're not eating."

She'd been making a special effort to encourage Elizabeth to talk since she'd been coming, and Abel must have noticed. She hurriedly picked up her fork.

"I was just thinking that maybe we could do something to make Matt's room more cheerful since he spends so much time there. Is there anything in his bedroom that maybe could be moved down?"

Abel looked blank, as most Amish men would when confronted with the idea of decorating. "I don't think…"

"His bookcase." The words, coming from Elizabeth, were so surprising that Miriam had to look again to be sure it was she who had spoken. Normally she didn't say anything unless prompted.

"That's a gut idea," Miriam said quickly, willing to encourage Elizabeth no matter what she suggested. "Maybe he'd like to read in his spare time." *Instead of staring at the ceiling*, she added to herself.

Betsy, who'd come back to join them once Matt was finished, seemed torn between discouraging the idea because it was Miriam's and trying to cheer her mammi.

Before she could decide, Miriam plunged into involving her. "What do you think, Betsy? Would we be able to bring the bookcase down between the two of us?"

"Yah, for sure."

She'd apparently decided to be encouraging. She

wouldn't want to suggest there was anything she couldn't handle.

"Actually," she continued, "I could bring it myself if I took the books out first. You don't need to help me."

Miriam just smiled. "I'd like to help. We'll have to decide where to put it. Any ideas?"

"What if we moved the sewing machine?" Once appealed to, Betsy seemed to be all in with the idea. "We could put it in the dining room. We don't use the dining room unless a lot of people are here, I mean, like…"

Like the day of David's funeral, Miriam finished for her. That would have been the last time there were many people in this house.

Elizabeth didn't move, but she seemed to retreat into herself, and Betsy looked stricken and guilty. Miriam reached out under the table to pat the girl's hand in sympathy. She hadn't meant any harm.

"Yah, a gut idea," Abel said firmly. "You girls can do that after you eat. I must hurry. Joshua is coming to help me finish the fencing."

Joshua, after consulting with Daad, had agreed to start working daily, but on the days of the early trip to the co-op, he usually went home for a few hours afterward. To sleep, Miriam thought. Like most boys his age, he always seemed to need sleep.

Elizabeth had slipped away from the table after eating hardly enough to keep a bird alive. Miriam looked after her, concerned. She'd make herself sick if she kept that up.

Miriam joined Betsy in clearing away after lunch. "Shall we go ahead and wash the dishes?" She'd always found washing dishes together conducive to sharing. Anything that made Betsy cooperative was certain sure worth doing. She didn't want to be struggling against Betsy, as well as Matthew.

"Let's do the bookcase first," Betsy said, looking eager. "I want to see his face when we take it in."

"Okay. I'll follow you." She'd been upstairs in the King house, but not for years. Had Matt been sharing a room with David? She didn't know.

But when Betsy led the way in, it seemed clear that this was Matt's alone. Like most Amish bedrooms, the room contained only necessary items. Matt's clothes hung on pegs on the wall, along with his winter felt hat and several pairs of suspenders. The shoes he didn't have a reason to wear now were lined up beneath the clothes, and Miriam's throat tightened at the sight.

Otherwise, a chest of drawers that would hold everything else he needed stood against the wall opposite the twin bed that was topped by one of Elizabeth's creations—a beautiful sunshine-and-shadows quilt in shades ranging from pale yellow to orange and rust and brown. It was like looking at the hillside in autumn.

Betsy was already kneeling in front of a two-shelf bookcase that stood beneath the window. Miriam hurried to join her. She pulled out an armload of books.

"It's the *Little House* books." Betsy sounded intrigued, as if she'd like to dip into them again herself. "Mammi read those to us when we were small."

"You liked the one about the Big Woods best."

Betsy jumped in reaction at finding her mother standing behind them. "And David…" Elizabeth stopped, struggling for a moment. "David liked…" Again she stopped.

Betsy brushed away a tear almost angrily. "He liked the prairie one. He wanted to hear it over and over."

Elizabeth's tears were flowing now, and to Miriam's surprise, she didn't freeze into herself again. Surely it was better for her to express her emotion rather than pretend it wasn't there.

"Yah," Elizabeth whispered. "He loved it." She moved blindly over to the chest, her back to them.

Betsy was busy stacking books to clear the bookcase, so Miriam picked up the first of several carved wooden animals arranged on top. "Should we take these downstairs, too?" She held up a very life-like bear.

Betsy looked up. "Yah, I guess. He made that one last winter."

"Matt did?" She hadn't thought Matt had an interest in anything that required sitting still.

Betsy nodded, standing up. "Okay, it's empty. Let's take it down. I'll go backwards."

She suspected that Betsy meant that she didn't trust Miriam to take the more difficult part of the job, but she ignored the jab, if that's what it was. Her mind revolved around this new facet of Matt's personality. Maybe it was one that would help his healing, if only she could approach it in the right way. She had to consider that and maybe even talk to Tim about it.

Matt stretched tired muscles and relaxed back against the pillow behind him. He hadn't realized how much it was going to take to live up to his promise about exercising. But he'd do it, if only to prove that he was right. He could pull on those stretchy bands all Miriam wanted, but at the end of the month, he'd still be unable to do any of the things he used to. Then Miriam would give up and go home.

For just a second, his conviction wavered. Having Miriam pop in and out to pester him did make the days go a little faster. Still, it didn't change things. He was useless. He'd been able to do the work of two men without tiring, and now he tired out pulling a couple of elastic bands.

He gritted his teeth. If he could take David's place in the accident right now, he'd do it in an instant.

Realizing he'd tensed his muscles again, Matt forced himself to relax. He couldn't rest all keyed up. If he could stop his thoughts from going round and round, maybe he'd even be able to take a nap.

He used to think naps were for babies. Now they were a prize to get him through the days.

Something thudded out in the hallway, followed by a spate of giggles, no doubt from Betsy. She used to giggle all the time, but he hadn't heard the sound since the accident. Now there was a scrape of wood against wood.

"Ouch, not so fast." Laughter threaded Miriam's voice, too, and someone bumped against the wall.

"What are you doing out there?" He shoved himself up against the pillow, thoughts of his nap evaporating. "Sounds like the house is coming down."

The door popped open, and his sister backed in. She

turned a laughing face toward him and knocked whatever she was carrying against the door.

"Wait and see," she said. "If Miriam quits steering me the wrong way."

"You're the one who's steering," Miriam retorted, pushing the door back with her elbow.

It was the bookcase from his bedroom that they were manhandling between them. "What are you doing with that? It belongs in my bedroom."

"We thought it might be more useful down here for now." Miriam swung her end of the bookcase around, and they settled it against the wall close to the bed. "This way you can have your books handy to read. In between exercising, of course."

Miriam's cheeks were flushed with the effort, and her blue eyes sparkled. Betsy had lost her sulky look, and she wiped her forehead with one hand still grinning.

"Whew. It's hot for furniture moving, yah? I'll get the first load of books before I melt."

"I don't want…" he began, but Betsy was already gone.

Miriam lifted her eyebrows in a question. "You don't want what?"

"I don't want my furniture moved around. You can just take that right back where it belongs."

Miriam plopped down on the chair Mammi used at the sewing machine. "I don't think I can. Not until I rest a little. What's wrong with having it down here?"

Nothing, except that it was your idea, he thought. "I don't want anything changed."

He probably sounded as stubborn as a child, but it was true. There was no sense in changing things around, making even more trouble for the family because of him. He'd caused enough problems.

Miriam met his gaze with a firmness that seemed new to the girl he remembered. She must have learned that during her home nursing. He didn't like it.

"If you're right, you won't need a bedroom upstairs, ain't so? Your mamm can use it for something else. Maybe for her quilting, ain't so? But if I'm right…well, Betsy and I will be wonderful happy to take everything back upstairs for you."

Betsy came in, laboring under an armload of books. She plopped it down next to the bookcase, and she and Miriam both dived in, starting to put books on the shelves.

"Do you want the books arranged by author?" Miriam, engrossed in what she was doing, barely glanced his way.

"I want…" he began, and realized there was no use in telling them again that he didn't want anything changed. Once Betsy had the bit between her teeth, she wouldn't quit. But he knew well enough who'd inspired this business. He glared at Miriam. "Yah, I guess if you're so set on doing it."

He was tempted to say he wouldn't be reading them anyway, but he wasn't so sure that was true, now that he thought about it. Reading might pass the time better than staring at the ceiling.

The two girls chattered away about books for a few minutes, and then Betsy went off to get another load.

He glanced at Miriam again and realized she was putting his carved animals on top of the bookcase.

"Don't bother with those. They're not good enough for anybody to see."

"Too late. I've already seen them." She held up the bear that he'd made last winter during the long evenings. "I love this one. You really made him look menacing."

"Would have been great if that was what I'd intended."

He hadn't meant it to be funny, but when he saw the laughter in her eyes, he couldn't help smiling , too.

"Let's say the bear wanted to be that way," she said, getting up. "Right?" She turned her head at voices from the kitchen. "Sounds like someone has come to visit. Shall I see who it is?"

But he'd already recognized one of the voices. "I don't want to see them." He must have sounded as panicked as he felt, because Miriam's eyes widened. "Hurry and stop them."

"But if it's someone who wants to see you—"

"No!" He all but shouted it. "For once will you do what I tell you?"

Her face paled at the anger he couldn't control. "Yah, for sure. Don't worry."

Miriam scurried out, probably glad to get away from him, and closed the door behind her. He grasped the edge of the hospital bed so hard the metal felt hot under his hands. Would she stop them?

The murmur of voices got louder for a moment, and his jaw clenched. If he could just lock the door, he'd be safe, but he couldn't get to it. He was helpless…helpless to avoid all the people he didn't want to see, and more importantly, that he didn't want to see him.

Miriam stood for a moment with her hands behind her on the door to Matt's room. Whoever was in the kitchen, Matt definitely didn't want them to visit him. Was he like that with everyone? Or was this someone special? She didn't think she'd ever seen him quite so desperate, and his feelings had touched her without words.

No matter who had come, it was up to her to turn the visitors away, she supposed. She doubted that Elizabeth could muster enough firmness. She headed for the kitchen, trying to remind herself that she was the one in charge of the sickroom now.

The two women who'd come in seemed to fill up the kitchen with their movement and chatter. Miriam hadn't pinpointed the voices, but she knew the women now that she saw them, just as she knew every person in the church district. Liva Ann Miller and her mother, Dora. No wonder it seemed so noisy in here—they were two of the most talkative women she'd ever met.

"Ach, here's Miriam, back from Ohio after such a long time!" Dora swept over to her for a quick embrace, her cheek not quite touching Miriam's. "Look, Liva Ann, it's Miriam. You're helping out, ain't so, Miriam?"

Miriam took breath to answer, but Dora surged on. "We heard you were back, and I said to Liva Ann, depend on it, Liva Ann, Miriam Stoltzfus will be helping out with Matthew, and sure enough, here you are."

"Yah, it's nice to see you, Miriam." But Liva Ann was looking right past her toward the door to Matt's room. "Such a gut thing you're here. I know you're a big help to dear Elizabeth. We brought a pineapple upside down cake. That's Matt's favorite, and I made it just for him. I'll go in—"

She took a step toward the hall, but Miriam moved to block her way. "I'm afraid that's impossible just now." She tried to emulate the tones of the visiting nurse she'd met out in Ohio—calm, pleasant, but admitting no argument.

"Oh, but Matt will want to see me. And the cake." Liva Ann held it up as if it were a pass to get into the room.

Miriam shook her head, smiling. She darted a glance at Elizabeth, but she looked helpless. And Betsy, who could probably stand up to anyone, had chosen this moment to disappear.

"I'm sure he'll love it, and his mamm will make sure he has some for dessert tonight. Right now he's resting. He's on a strict schedule, you know, for meals and therapy and rest."

"Ach, he can't be sleeping, not with the noise we're making." Dora laughed heartily. "My grossmammi always did say, 'Dora, your laugh is loud enough to call the cows home from pasture,' and she certain sure was nice. Just give Liva Ann a peep in the door. A look at her pretty face is sure to cheer him up—"

"Not now." Miriam was shaking inside, but she

stood firm. "We'll tell him all about your visit." She tried to vie with Dora's endless line of chatter. "It was *sehr gut* of you to come."

Seizing the cake and putting it on the table, she shepherded them toward the door, making sure Liva Ann didn't dart around her. "His therapy session is scheduled in half an hour, and we must get ready. So nice to see you both."

"But—" Dora began, but Elizabeth, apparently stirred into life by the prospect of getting rid of them, had opened the door. Miriam, arms spread wide to corral them, ushered them out.

"Goodbye. Greet your family for me." She closed the door and held on to the latch for a moment, half-afraid they would attempt another entry.

But Liva Ann was tugging at her mother. "Come on. I told you he didn't want to see me. You never listen to me. Let's go home."

Miriam stood at the screen door, watching the buggy carrying Liva Ann Miller and her mother turn onto the main road and disappear. Liva Ann's words to her mother had been odd. If she hadn't seen Matt, how did she know he didn't want to see her?

With a sigh of relief that they were gone, she glanced at Elizabeth, who sank down onto a seat at the table. Betsy, who'd appeared with another armload of books too late to help, patted her mother's shoulder.

"What was all this?" Miriam asked. "Why was Matt so…so frantic about not seeing them?"

It was Betsy who answered her. "Didn't you know

about Liva Ann? Matt was courting her before the accident."

Miriam shook her head, a little surprised at that pairing. "I was in Ohio at my aunt's for most of the last year, remember? I'm pretty sure nobody mentioned it in the letters I got."

She considered Matt's visitors. Easy enough to see what attracted him to Liva Ann, with her huge brown eyes fringed by long lashes and her pink cheeks. With the purple dress she wore, her coloring made her look like a pansy.

Matt had recognized Liva Ann's voice, all right. And he hadn't wanted to see her.

"But if they were courting…" She pushed away the reflection that Liva Ann was awfully young for him. "Hasn't he seen her at all since the accident?" She asked the question of Betsy, but surprisingly it was Elizabeth who answered.

"No, not once. She came to the hospital, but he wouldn't see her. We thought maybe when he was at home, he'd change his mind." Her voice shook a little on the words. "If only he'd see her…"

"He won't." Betsy sounded scornful. "Why would he? All Liva Ann ever thinks about is how pretty she is."

"Betsy, that's not kind." Elizabeth roused herself to scold. "She's just…" She couldn't seem to find the word, so Miriam filled in for her.

"Immature?" She actually thought Betsy had described Liva Ann very well, but she ought not say so.

"I suppose." Elizabeth frowned down at her hands,

pressed on the tabletop. "She's not what I would have chosen for him," she burst out as if relieved to say the words. "But I'd be glad for anyone who would help him."

Miriam didn't say anything. At least today's events seemed to be bringing Elizabeth out of the cold shell she'd been inhabiting.

As for Liva Ann, it seemed doubtful that someone as young and frivolous as she was would be of much help in this situation, but maybe she was wrong. Besides, maybe what Matt needed was someone pretty and flirtatious who'd distract him from his troubles.

If he refused to see her, well, he had his reasons.

Elizabeth looked at her almost pleadingly. "Don't you think it would be good for him to see her? Maybe, if you talked to him…"

"I don't think he'd listen to me," she said hurriedly. But then, because Elizabeth was looking at her so pleadingly, she added, "If…if I see a way to do it, I'll encourage him. All right?"

Elizabeth actually came close to a smile at that. "Denke," she whispered.

It was a good thing she couldn't see the reluctance Miriam felt to do any such thing. As for Miriam…well, she really didn't want to look too closely into her reasons for not encouraging their romance.

Chapter Four

On Sunday morning, Miriam was up before dawn, along with the rest of the family. Everyone had to move even earlier on worship Sundays, since the cows had to be taken care of, breakfast cooked and eaten, everyone cleaned up and ready to leave for the drive to the farm where worship was being held.

The older boys had matured enough over the past year that no one had to help them...except for trying to get Joshua away from the mirror. As for the three youngest ones, they dallied around, finding every excuse to be late, until Mamm raised her voice. Then they were suddenly ready and waiting.

Mammi exchanged exasperated looks with Miriam as she shepherded her brood out to the buggy. "If they could do it after I shouted, why couldn't they do it before?"

"Is it any comfort to know that they will eventually grow up?" Miriam reached out to disentangle the twins, who were trying to climb into the buggy at the same time.

"I'll be too old to care by then," Mammi muttered, and then broke into smile. "Just you wait and see."

Shaking her head, Miriam climbed in after her. Once again, very carefully, Mammi was hinting about the grandchildren she'd like to have. It seemed more and more unlikely to Miriam that she'd be able to provide any of them.

The buggy reached the end of the lane, and Daad stopped to let Abel King's buggy go past, carrying only him and Betsy. Mammi shook her head as they pulled in behind.

"Poor Elizabeth. I'd be wonderful glad to stay with Matthew so she could go to worship, but she keeps saying no."

Miriam patted her mother's hand. "I know. I would, too, but I'm afraid she's not ready to go anywhere. It's a challenge even to get her out in the garden."

Mammi shook her head. "All we can do now is pray for them and wait."

That was probably so, although Miriam knew Mammi would rather do something more active to solve the problem. She understood… It was how she felt, too.

By the time they had gone two miles, they'd caught up with a long line of Amish buggies moving in the same direction. Miriam found something almost prayerful in that steady progress of the community toward worship, and she knew the others did, as well. Even the twins stopped squabbling in the back seat.

Worship was at the home of her cousin Lyddy's family today, so she would have a chance to spend time with Grossmammi, who lived with them. She hadn't seen enough of her since she'd returned. Or of her female cousins, Lyddy and Beth.

Miriam felt a burst of excitement at the thought of her cousins. They wouldn't have much chance to talk until after worship, but surely at some point today they'd be able to catch up. She might not have sisters, but her two cousins were just as close. They'd known each other since they were babies, often in the same playpen, and the round-robin letters they'd exchanged while she was away didn't make up for talking in person.

When they reached the farm, Sammy hopped down to join the other boys who were serving as hostlers today, taking care of the horses and buggies. John Thomas, the bolder of the eight-year-old twins, tugged at Mammi's sleeve.

"Can we sit with the other boys today, Mammi? Please?" He asked the question every worship Sunday, but Mamm and Daad hadn't shown signs of weakening yet.

Her mother touched his cheek. "Not today. Soon Daadi and I will have a talk about it."

John Thomas opened his mouth to argue, but Miriam caught his eye and shook her head at him. Would John Thomas ever learn that it wasn't a good idea to argue back? Probably not. Miriam gave him a consoling pat as she stepped down.

"Soon," she said. "It will take longer if you argue."

He didn't look entirely convinced, and his lower lip protruded, but then a smile warmed his blue eyes, and he tugged at his twin's hand. "Come on, James. Don't be so slow."

Miriam glanced toward the barn, where folks were already lining up for worship, women on one side, men on the other. There was a low murmur of voices from the men, but on the women's side, the murmur rose to a buzz. Miriam caught several people looking at her, and her stomach seemed to turn over.

They couldn't have heard anything about what happened in Ohio, could they? Surely not. Her relatives wouldn't talk about it.

Her mother nudged her forward. "We'd best get lined up."

Miriam froze for a moment and then moved automatically. "Mammi, people are staring at me." She kept her voice to a whisper but still looked around to be sure no one heard.

Her mother's calm glance seemed to take in all her thoughts and fears. "They're just happy to see you home again, ain't so? Komm."

Telling herself she was too sensitive and Mammi was right, Miriam moved on toward the place where younger women stood in the line. But if she was convinced, why were her fingers clenched so that her nails dented her palm?

Her cousin Lyddy, standing with the oldest of the unmarried women, wiggled her fingers at Miriam. Lyddy would be moving up to the married women soon, since she'd be marrying Simon Fisher sometime this fall. It hadn't been announced yet, but anyone who saw them looking at each other across the width of the barn would know it.

Lyddy clasped her hand when she slipped into place next to her. Her cousin Beth, a couple of places away from them with the married women, reached back to touch her hand, smiling.

A year older than Miriam, Beth had been married and widowed before she was twenty, but now she wore a contented glow of happiness after her remarriage. Miriam was the only one left who hadn't found somebody to love.

She chased the thought away. She had a full life without marriage, didn't she?

Her thoughts flickered back to the memories of what had happened out west, and her muscles seemed to tighten in response. She'd filled her life with service to others, especially those who were recovering from illness or injury. She couldn't let one failure ruin everything.

A hush fell over those waiting as the lines began to move. The barn where she had played so often as a child would have been cleaned and cleaned again in preparation for worship. This couldn't totally eliminate the scent of a barn, but somehow that seemed right, too. They worshiped in the spaces where they lived and worked, because worship was part of daily life.

Once they were inside, and she was seated next to Lyddy, Miriam's sense of being watched seemed to vanish. Grossmammi, seated two rows behind her with Mammi, sent one of her sweet smiles toward her, and farther down the row, Anna Schmidt, who'd been their teacher in school ages ago, smiled and waved.

As the vorsinger sang the first notes of the familiar first hymn, Miriam relaxed and lifted her voice. She was home, where she was loved and cherished. No one would think badly of her here, would they?

It wasn't until she was alone with Lyddy and Beth in the farmhouse kitchen after lunch that the subject of her visit to Ohio came up.

"So, how is Aunt Etta?" Lyddy asked, plunging a platter into the hot water in the sink. "I guess recovering from a hip operation is no fun."

"No, it's not, but you know how Aunt Etta is…always laughing and joking no matter what happens."

Aunt Etta was not actually their aunt—really a second or third cousin, she supposed—but in the wide-ranging genealogy of the Amish, she was family. She belonged to their parents' generation, so it seemed natural to refer to her that way.

Miriam smiled at the memory of her patient. "As soon as the physical therapist started her on exercises, there was no holding her. My job ended up being to keep her from doing too much."

"A bit different from working with Matthew King, I guess." Beth seized the platter to dry before Miriam could reach it. "I've heard he's being…well, difficult. I'm not criticizing," she added quickly, and no one looking at her sweet face could think it. "It must be terrible, losing his brother that way."

Miriam nodded. She always tried not to talk about

the people she thought of as her patients, but it was natural for folks who knew the family to be concerned.

"Yah, it's hard for him to focus on his own healing when he's grieving David." She thought briefly of her bargain with Matthew, wondering again if she'd done the right thing. "But he has been working with the physical therapist well enough."

"And not so much with you?" Lyddy said, her eyes twinkling.

"Well…he's not as wholehearted about it as I'd like." She was silent for a moment, overwhelmed by her need to help Matthew for his own sake, but also for hers. If she failed him the way she'd failed young Wayne…

She tried to force the thought away, but her eyes filled with tears. The dish Lyddy was washing clattered in the sink, and in an instant both of them had their arms around Miriam.

"What is it, Miriam? I knew something was wrong when you came back all of a sudden like that." Beth dried her tears gently with the corner of a tea towel.

"You can tell us." Lyddy patted her shoulder. "You know that."

Yes, Miriam knew it, and she realized she'd had this at the back of her mind all morning. She never had been able to keep anything from her cousins, and they'd never failed her.

She sniffed and wiped her eyes with her fingers. "I was going to come back as soon as Aunt Etta was better, but you know how it is…they kept wanting me to stay. I'd finally made arrangements to leave, but then another family in the church district asked if I could help them for a time. They have a boy, only fifteen, Wayne."

She seemed to see the pale, thin boy, his joints so painful he could hardly move, his face drooping with sorrow. "He has what they call an autoimmune disease. Sometimes he'd be fine, but then he'd go downhill again, and he was having a bad spell right then. They needed someone who could take over for the mother for a few weeks, stay with him, help him with his exercises and treatments."

"So you said yes." Beth said the obvious thing.

Miriam nodded, her throat tightening. "Poor boy, not able to do what every other teenager took for granted. I was glad to help."

Lyddy patted her shoulder. "Something went wrong, yah?"

"Yah." She hesitated, but she needed to say it. "I didn't realize he…he was getting attached to me." She swallowed with difficulty. "Too attached. He thought he was in love, thought…well, all kinds of things that weren't real. And it all exploded when I finally realized and tried to talk to him about it."

Beth put her arm around Miriam's waist. "It wasn't your fault," she said firmly, and Lyddy nodded.

"It *was* my fault," she said, angry at herself. "I should have seen. If only I had realized sooner…but I didn't, and there was a scene. His mother said terrible things about me. Wayne was so upset. If I could have talked to him, maybe I could have helped. But his parents wouldn't listen. They were sure it was all my fault. They said I'd made him even worse."

Her voice choked with tears. She couldn't say anything else, but she didn't need to. They hugged her and
wiped away her tears, and Beth said loving things while
Lyddy said silly things just to make her laugh instead
of cry, like always.

Finally Miriam mopped her face again. "Ach, it was
silly for me to fall apart like that." She gave them a
thankful look. "But I'm glad I did. I wrote to Mamm
and Daad about it, but that's different from actually
saying it out loud."

How strange that was, but it was true. Just saying
the words aloud was sort of like removing a painful
thorn—it hurt, but at least maybe then it could heal.

Beth hugged her again. "You have to put it behind
you. You couldn't have known what would happen.
What does your mother say?"

"She thinks I should just talk about it openly to
people. After all, folks here are bound to learn about it
through relatives out there. She says it would be easier."

"Well, then, that's what you should do." Lyddy's way
was to charge at any problem. Miriam had known that
would be her advice.

"I know, I know. You're right, and Mammi's right,
but I just can't do it. Well, look at me—I'm falling
apart just telling you."

"Don't you think it will be easier once people
know?" Beth asked gently.

"I guess."

"After all, you said this was the first time you'd really talked about it." Beth was quietly persuasive, as
always.

Miriam nodded, but as relieved as she felt, she didn't really agree. She should have known, shouldn't have been so confident she could help. And she just couldn't go around talking to people about it.

Well, there was no danger of her being overconfident now. She didn't have any confidence left.

The sound of a footstep on the back porch shocked her into awareness of her state. Someone was coming, and here she was with her eyes probably swollen and her face tearstained.

"I can't let anyone see me like this," she gasped.

Lyddy was already pulling her toward the hall. "In the pantry, quick, and shut the door. We'll get rid of whoever it is."

"It's all right," Beth whispered. "Go."

Miriam hurried around the corner and into the pantry. She got the door closed just in time, but she could still hear the voices in the kitchen. Hear and recognize. It was Hilda Berger, and Hilda was well known across the county for the way everything she thought came out of her mouth. Without a pause to consider, some said.

Miriam hugged herself and prayed Hilda wasn't looking for something in the pantry.

"But I made sure Miriam would be in here with the two of you," Hilda exclaimed. "I haven't had a chance to talk with her since she came home from Ohio. I have some kinfolk out there, you know. Maybe she even met them while she was there."

Miriam closed her eyes and hoped for the best. The shelf full of canned applesauce pressed against her back.

"She was here earlier," Beth said vaguely.

"You'll catch up with her, I'm sure." Lyddy, a little bolder, spoke out. "Maybe you can find her with her family."

"Yah, I guess you're right." She must have moved toward the door, because the sound faded a little. "Ach, I'm forgetting why I came. I'm supposed to take out another quart of applesauce from the pantry." Her voice had become louder, and Miriam slid behind the door, patting her face in the hope it would chase away the traces of tears.

There were rapid footsteps, and a hand brushed the door. "I'll get it for you, Hilda." Lyddy must be right outside.

In another instant, the knob turned. Miriam grabbed a quart of the applesauce, and when Lyddy moved, Miriam thrust it into her hand. Lyddy grabbed it, still talking, and seemed to steer Hilda away.

Miriam closed the door silently and leaned on it, eyes closed. She knew who Hilda's relatives were—her Aunt Etta had introduced them. Even if Hilda could be avoided, it wouldn't help. Hilda's cousin was even more of a chatterer than Hilda was. There was no chance at all that she wouldn't tell Hilda all about it. And what Hilda knew, everyone would know.

By the time of Miriam's late arrival on Monday morning, Matt had worked himself into a bad mood. It wasn't that he wanted her here or looked forward to her company. He'd be just as happy to see her quit. But if she took on a job, she ought to be on time.

He'd been awake since five. He'd heard Miriam's brother and Daad talking outside as they loaded the wagon to take vegetables to the co-op. August was the busiest month on the farm—sweet corn, tomatoes, peppers—they were all at their peak now. And he couldn't help. He had to lie here and listen to someone else doing his work.

When Miriam tapped, his answering shout no doubt told her that he was irritated. She came in, closely followed by Betsy, who seemed to think she had to keep an eye on him, as if he were a toddler.

"You're late."

Miriam looked at him, and her expression startled him. It was almost as if her thoughts were so far away that she didn't even register his sharp comment. Then she blinked, and her clear blue eyes focused on him.

"I'm sorry. I've no good reason, except that I ran into Joshua outside." A smile touched her lips and was reflected in her eyes. "He had to tell me all about how many dozens of ears of sweet corn they took to market this morning. According to him, people were lined up waiting to get at it when they'd barely finished unloading."

Her voice seemed to fade as she reached the end of what she was saying, as if she sensed his mood. But she couldn't know she'd touched a sore spot.

"Josh likes his job, does he?" He made an effort to put some enthusiasm into his voice.

Seeming reassured, she nodded. "He says he feels like an outsider in the family, thinking more of crops than of cows. But I know Daad's okay with it."

He couldn't help smiling at that thought. Still, Miriam's daad had other sons ready and eager to run the dairy business, unlike his own.

Miriam reached up to pull down the cables he was supposed to use to sit up and eventually, so Tim said, allow him to get into a wheelchair on his own. Matt gritted his teeth. "You're not going to start with that, are you?"

She looked surprised. "Why not?" She glanced up again. "Although if I can't reach them, they're not going to do much good. How did they get up so high?"

"I didn't like them dangling over me. I told Betsy to get them out of the way."

"Maybe Betsy can get..."

Before she could finish the thought, Betsy turned away. "I think Mammi's calling me." In another moment she was gone.

Miriam looked after her, shrugged and picked up the stool that stood against the wall. "What does Betsy have against being helpful?"

"Nothing," he said quickly, trying not to feel embarrassed. "I guess she knows I don't like that exercise much."

"All the more reason to get it over with first," she said, putting the stool next to the bed and stepping up. "Ain't so? My grossmammi always says to do the hardest thing first and the rest of the day will be good."

"Your grandmother never had to waste time on something that..." His complaint withered and died when he looked up at Miriam.

She was leaning against the bed for balance as she

reached above her head for the handles. She'd been close to him before—she could hardly help it when she worked with him. But he'd never had this kind of a look at her before. Sunlight streaming in the east window brought out golden highlights in the hair he'd always thought mousy. Her position, arms raised, outlined her slender figure, and her cheeks were flushed with the effort, making him think of ripe peaches.

"I guess we could shorten the exercises this morning," she said as she climbed down, pulling the handles to their full length. "After all, Tim will give you a hefty workout this afternoon." She looked at him again. "Matt?"

Brought back to the moment, he shook his head, trying to banish her image from his mind. "Nope. I can't have you saying I'm not living up to my part of the bargain. Do your worst."

That surprised her into a smile that lightened her expression. "I'll do my best," she corrected him. "And so will you." She put the handles in his hands, her touch sure and firm. "Let's do a few partial sit-ups."

As he rose up, pulling against the handles, she moved closer to put her palm on his back, helping him. He had control of himself now. He wasn't going to lose track of what he was doing because of Miriam.

But he found himself studying the curves of her face, only six inches or so from his. Was it his imagination that once again she didn't look quite as calm and peaceful as usual? He couldn't be sure.

"Something wrong at home?" he asked abruptly.

She blinked. "No, nothing. Not unless you count

Sammy finding new ways to risk life and limb and trying to get the twins to follow him in mischief."

"Sammy's what? Ten, now? He'll probably grow out of it."

"If he lives long enough," she said. "Between climbing to the barn roof and fighting with the goat, he has Mammi at her wits' end, she says."

He had to smile. It seemed, whatever the problem was, it wasn't at home. With his red hair and constant grin, Sammy had always looked...not for trouble, he guessed, but for things that seemed to lead him into it. Anyway, why should he care what had put that worried look in her eyes?

They moved on through another set of exercises, and he couldn't rid himself of the thought. What was distracting her? It shouldn't bother him, but it did.

"How was worship yesterday?" The question popped out without his thinking about it, but in an instant he saw that it was the right one. Her hand tightened on his arm, seeming to communicate without words.

In another moment, her face smoothed out. "Fine. It was gut to see the familiar faces again. I missed all of you while I was away."

The words were the right ones, but the feeling beneath them wasn't, he felt sure. He studied her face, searching for answers.

Miriam seemed to feel his scrutiny, and she shrugged as if to shake it off.

"That wasn't very convincing," he said. "You want to try a different response?" She could tell him to mind his own business, but he didn't think she would.

Looking down, she stared at the soft exercise ball she was squashing between her fingers. Finally she shook her head. "I was glad to see everyone, but by the time I'd answered the same questions about my time in Ohio twenty or so times, I guess I was a little tired of it."

"They're just trying to catch up, ain't so? You didn't get up to anything out there you have to hide, did you?"

He expected her to either deny it or turn it off with a joke. Instead, she went completely still, her eyes dark with pain. In another moment, she was shaking her head and smiling.

"Not a bit of it," she said, her voice light.

But it was too late. He knew what he'd seen. Pain.

Chapter Five

Miriam arrived at the King place Tuesday morning to find Abel waiting on the back porch steps. He stood up as she approached, nodding in his grave way. Was he waiting for her to hear her report from the therapist's visit the previous day? Anyone could see at a glance how heavy a burden Abel carried, but he had hope, even so.

"I'd be glad to talk with you a moment, Miriam." He hesitated. "It's about Joshua."

Miriam rearranged her thoughts as quickly as possible. She hadn't expected that, and a flash of concern went through her. Was he going to say that Josh wasn't living up to expectations?

"Yah, of course." She tried to hide her concern with a smile. "I hope he's doing all right."

"Ach, yah, more than all right." For an instant the lines in Abel's face seemed to relax. "I was wondering… I would speak to your daad first, but I thought you might know. If he has plans for Joshua, I wouldn't say anything, that's for sure."

The more Abel said, the more confused she felt. "Plans? Do you mean for today?"

He actually laughed a little at that, shaking his head. "I'm that ferhoodled, I'm saying it backwards. Josh has been a wonderful gut help to me. I wondered if he would want to make his job more permanent. But if your daad has something else in mind for him…"

There was a tentative note in his words that she began to understand. What would the future of the farm be without Matthew and David? She hesitated, not wanting to speak for anyone else, although she did know that Josh was happy with his work.

"I haven't heard Daad say anything about it. I expect he knows Josh's heart isn't in the dairy business, though. He knows most things."

Abel nodded. "You know how I'm fixed without David and not knowing how much Matthew will come back." His voice choked on the words, and he looked as if he regretted starting this talk.

"Yah, I know. I'm sorry," she said hastily. "It's hard to make any plans, not knowing. But you can be sure Josh is happy here, and if you want to talk to him about…well, anything, I feel sure Daad wouldn't mind."

Her heart hurt for Abel, and for an instant she had an unreasonable anger with the boy who'd been so reckless. If he had known how many lives his foolishness was going to affect, would he have believed it?

"Gut, gut." Abel seemed satisfied with what was really only half an answer to his question. "I was sorry to miss Tim when he was here yesterday. Has he said anything about Matt's progress?"

He looked so in need of hope that Miriam would have done anything to reassure him. "It's early days yet, you know. The damage to Matthew's legs…well, the doctor would talk to you about it, I'm sure. Tim talks in terms of what we should do this week, or maybe next week."

She was running out of optimistic things to say, and it was almost a relief when the screen door slammed open. Betsy stood there, scowling at her.

"Matt wants to know why you're not in there working."

"Betsy." Abel didn't raise his voice, but it was stern enough to send Betsy back a step. "You will not speak that way to Miriam or anyone else."

Betsy's expression became mulish. "Matt said—"

"You heard me."

Miriam wondered for a moment if he'd scold his older son. Probably not, even though the words were probably his.

"I'll come now," she said cheerfully. "Unless you wanted to say anything more?"

"No. Denke, Miriam. That was helpful." Abel turned away, his thoughts obviously running ahead to the work to be done. She didn't suppose it was really very helpful, but what could she say? What could anyone say about how much Matt would recover?

Betsy managed to slam the screen door again when she went inside, and Miriam opened it gingerly, hoping the hinges would hold up. Reminding herself that Betsy was dealing with a lot of changes in her young life, she resolved to be pleasant. Or at least, patient with her.

"What were you and Daad talking about outside?" Matt demanded the moment she went into his room.

She should have been prepared so she wouldn't be standing there like the dressmaker's dummy Mammi fitted dresses on. She didn't want to be the one to say his daad was thinking of bringing Joshua in permanently. It would be like telling him he was never going to recover.

In the end she replied with part of the truth. "He was sorry to have missed Tim yesterday and wanted to know what he said."

"Well, what did he say? You and Tim were a long time in the kitchen yesterday. Or was that a social visit?"

Matt seemed to be in as bad a mood as Betsy. Still, he had a bit more of an excuse for it. Ignoring his implication about her and Tim was the only way to handle it.

"Just the usual discussion of plans for the week." She released the brake of the wheelchair and rolled it closer, then picked up the stool and carried it over to the side of the bed.

"And what are those plans?" Matt eyed her preparations warily.

Maybe it would have been better for Tim to have discussed it with Matt. Miriam put some enthusiasm into her voice. "Tim thinks we should work on your ability to get into the wheelchair on your own." At the rejection on his lips, she held up her hand. "Not right away. I just brought the wheelchair over to give you an idea of how it's done."

"I'm not trying to get into that thing with just you to help me. We'd both end up on the floor."

Relieved at the trace of humor in his voice, she smiled. "It's the goal. We're just taking steps toward it." She got up on the stool, leaning against the edge of the bed. "And Tim says you should start going out to the kitchen to join the family for meals."

His reply was quick and sharp. "No." He glared at her. "You think I want to take away everyone's appetite?"

Miriam looked down on him from her perch, honestly baffled for a moment. And then she realized he was talking about his scarred face—the scarring she didn't even see any longer. Maybe it was time to see what scolding would do.

"Don't be ferhoodled," she snapped. "Nobody minds that. And for some reason I don't understand at the moment, they really want to enjoy your company while they eat. Must have something to do with loving you, I suppose."

She stretched up, reaching for the handles that seemed to be completely entangled. A quick glance back at him showed him looking equal parts surprised and embarrassed at her words. Well, that was good. He ought to be embarrassed.

Her groping fingers touched the handles, and she stretched further to take a grip with both hands and pull. They didn't come. Exasperated, she looked up, giving them a good tug.

For an instant she thought she'd brought the whole ceiling down. The handles struck her face as she teetered off balance and then fell heavily, half on the bed, and her head struck the footboard.

"Look out!" Matt lunged forward as Miriam fell, but his muscles betrayed him. His hand fell short, and the sound of her head striking the footboard echoed in his head.

"Mamm! Daad!"

But already he heard footsteps pounding in the hall. The door flew open. Mammi and Daad rushed through, followed by Joshua and then Betsy.

Miriam moved, hand against her head, and he managed to grasp her sleeve. "Don't move. Not until my mother takes a look at you."

Mammi hurried to Miriam, putting one arm around her and tilting her head back gently. The lump on her forehead was growing larger and redder while he looked at it.

His mother clucked and stroked her forehead. "Hush, now, Miriam. It will be all right." She looked up and raised her voice. "Don't just stand there. Betsy, go and wet a dishtowel with cold water. Wring it out thoroughly and bring it. Someone move the rocking chair over here next to Miriam."

"I… I'm all right," Miriam murmured. "You don't need…"

"Just let me take care of you. Rest, now."

Daad carried the rocking chair, and Joshua rushed to help him, his face white. As they set it in place, Mat-

thew caught his father's eye and knew they were thinking the same thing. The woman snapping out orders
was Mammi the way she used to be, before tragedy
struck. It was wonderful good to hear her taking control again, even at the cost of a lump on Miriam's head.

"Denke, Elizabeth." Miriam's voice was weak, and
she allowed her brother to lift her from her awkward
position. He settled her gently in the rocking chair.

She patted his cheek. "I'm all right. Don't be upset."

"Who, me?" He managed a light tone, but it trembled a little. "I know how tough you are."

Her smile flickered. "What happened?" She was
looking at Matt now for answers. "It felt like the ceiling fell on me."

"Not quite. The hook holding the cords pulled
loose from the ceiling." Matt glanced toward the floor.
"Where did it go?"

Daad picked up the cords and handles from the bed,
making sure the hook wasn't there. Meanwhile Josh
scrambled on the floor in search of the hook, crawling under the bed.

"Here it is." He crawled backward from under the
bed, holding it up. "Funny it came out like that."

"Yah." Daad took it in a work-hardened hand, brushing off the bits of plaster that stuck to it. "I put it in
myself. It should have been able to hold Matt, let alone
a little thing like you, Miriam." He frowned, looking
from the hook to the hole in the ceiling. "I'm wonderful sorry, Miriam. That's certain sure. It's my fault."

Betsy had returned with the wet cloth and an extra
towel, and Mammi pressed it gently against Miriam's

forehead. "Denke, Betsy." Mamm was so focused on what she was doing that she didn't look up at Betsy.

But Matt did. He saw an expression on his sister's face that startled him. She wore a small, sly grin.

It disappeared when she spoke. "I guess you won't have to do those exercises today."

For a moment he didn't understand, and then he saw it. Betsy knew he always complained about those particular exercises. Maybe she'd decided on a way to keep him from having to do them.

No, that couldn't be true. She surely wouldn't have set out to hurt Miriam, would she?

He was frowning at his little sister, trying to figure it out, when she seemed to feel his eyes on her. The color came up in her face. She turned away quickly and had gotten a couple of steps toward the door when he spoke.

"Hold on, Betsy. What do you mean by that?"

She turned around slowly, and suddenly everyone was looking at her. He could see the moment at which she decided to bluff.

"What? I didn't mean anything." She must have seen the doubt in his gaze. "Really. I just thought you'd be glad…"

"Glad to have Miriam get hurt when she's trying to help me?" He had to muffle himself not to shout. "What was in your mind to do such a thing?"

"Betsy, is this true?" Daad looked as if someone had hit him, and Miriam was close enough to Matt that he could hear her sharp intake of breath.

For an instant longer Betsy held out. Then her expression seemed to crumble away. "I didn't," she protested. "I mean… I mean… I just untwisted the hook a little bit. I didn't mean for anyone to get hurt. Not Miriam, not anyone. I didn't think she would. I just… I just wanted to help Matt."

"*Help* me?" he repeated.

He felt the urge to shout again, but something stronger prevented him. Why was he blaming Betsy? What she said was true enough. He'd talked carelessly about hating those exercises and wishing he didn't have to do them. He looked aghast at the result of his stupidity. He should have known better.

Daad looked solemnly at Matt for a moment—long enough for Matt to hear the things he didn't say. Then he turned to Betsy.

"Miriam *was* hurt," Daad said soberly. "And you are responsible. I would never think a child of mine would do such a thing."

"But I didn't mean it. And anyway, Matt shouldn't have to do anything he doesn't want to." It was a feeble attempt at defiance, and she looked ready to cry.

Daad went on as if she hadn't spoken. "Go to your room, and don't come out until I say to. And while you're there, think about how you'll feel if you must go before the church and confess that you have injured a sister."

Betsy's face went white, and Miriam murmured an instinctive protest. But Daad's face said no argument would sway him. Betsy spun and fled. They heard her footsteps pounding up the stairs.

Miriam pushed herself up to standing…a little wobbly, but standing. Her face was very pale, and the red mark stood out like a light. She looked as if she wanted to say something about it to Daad, but Matt shook his head, and she subsided.

It would do no good now. Later, when Daad had cooled down, he'd speak to him.

Miriam seemed to understand his unspoken message. She moved closer to the bed. "We must get busy. There's no reason not to do the rest of the exercises now."

"Not until you've had a sit-down and a nice cup of tea." Mammi gathered herself together and took Miriam's arm. "Come along now."

Before Miriam could move, Matt closed his hand around her wrist. She looked at him, eyes wide and startled, and he could feel the pulse stuttering under her skin.

"I'm sorry," he said softly. "I should have known better than to complain in front of Betsy."

Miriam shook her head slightly and then stopped, touching her forehead as if it had been a bad idea. "It's all right." She let Mammi lead her away.

But it wasn't all right, and he knew it. He'd caused her injury as sure as if he'd done it himself. And what was just as bad, she'd fallen within inches of him and he couldn't help her. He was useless, totally useless.

Miriam sank into a kitchen chair, relieved to sit and be quiet for a moment. Elizabeth didn't speak as she hustled about the kitchen heating the kettle and getting out tea. Finally she set a brimming mug in front of Miriam and sank onto the chair at the end of the table.

"What else can I get for you? Some toast or a piece of shoofly pie?" She watched Miriam anxiously.

Miriam managed to give her a reassuring smile. "Nothing else, denke. I'm all right, really."

"I can't tell you how sorry I am for what Betsy did. I should have known, should have realized..." Her words broke on a sob.

"Ach, don't." Miriam clasped her hand, patting it. "I understand." At least, she thought she did. Betsy was trying desperately to claim her remaining brother, afraid of losing him the way she lost David.

Elizabeth sniffed and dabbed at her nose with a tissue. "If you understand, it's more than I do. That child..."

"Betsy's grieving," she said firmly, knowing that, at least, was true. "I'm sure she didn't mean to hurt me. She was just trying to help her brother." She hesitated, not wanting to open any sore places in poor Elizabeth's heart. "She is missing what her family used to be, ain't so?"

Looking at her, Elizabeth's attention seemed to be caught. "You think so? But what she did—"

She nodded, patting the older woman's hand again. "I've already forgiven her. I just wish I could do something more to help."

Elizabeth blinked away tears. "Denke, Miriam. I'm the one who must help her. I see it now."

Did she? Miriam sincerely hoped so. This whole family needed help, but it was more than she knew how to do. One good thing had come out of this morning's mishap, anyway. Elizabeth had awakened from her self-imposed isolation. If only this awareness would last... She murmured a silent prayer that it would be so.

She gulped down the rest of her tea, hearing a few thuds accompanied by the rumble of men's voices from Matt's room. "I must go. Matt should have at least a short exercise period this morning."

When she walked back into Matt's room, it was to find Matt sitting up on the bed, apparently supervising while his father and Josh finished installing the apparatus again.

"There," Josh said, attaching the end hooks that Abel handed to him. "All done."

He stepped down and grinned at Miriam. "I guarantee it won't come down again."

"And she'll know who to blame if it does," Matt said with a wink at him.

"Yah, just me." He pushed the stool back in place while Abel took the toolbox, and he looked over at Miriam. "We looped the cords over this hook above the bed, so you don't have to go climbing on anything. Give it a try."

Smiling at her little brother's obvious pleasure in his work, Miriam went over to the bed, finding that she could easily reach the handles and lift them off.

"Terrific. Denke."

Abel started for the door and then paused, looking at her. "Are you sure you wouldn't like to go home and rest? We can get along without you for the remainder of the day, if need be."

"Not at all. I'm ready to work, and so is Matthew."

Matt's lips quirked at her comment, but he didn't speak.

Joshua started to follow his boss, and then he detoured to give Miriam a quick hug before leaving. "Take care."

She stood looking as the door closed behind them, and then she turned to Matt, shaking her head. "I wouldn't have believed how much my little brother has changed in just the months I've been away."

"He's not so little anymore," Matt commented.

"Yah, but it's not just that. It's a change in himself. He was always so quiet and reserved that it was rare to know what he was thinking. Now...now he's talking to me about himself and not embarrassed at all."

"You're better friends now that he's growing up." His eyes were shadowed for a moment, and she guessed he was thinking about his brother.

"I'm sorry I missed some of the growing up." She considered those months when she was away. "I guess any change in the family affects all of them."

Matt studied her face, maybe trying to read what was behind her words. "That might be aimed at me, ain't so?"

She felt her cheeks grow warm. "I wasn't really thinking of that. Should I apologize?"

"Not necessary. It's right about us, too, and our change is a lot harder to deal with. Betsy...well, she shouldn't have done it, but I guess I can understand, a little."

Miriam nodded, relieved that, like his mother, he

was seeing a bit more clearly. "She really wants to hold on to you now."

"Maybe so." He didn't seem convinced. "Well, I've learned my lesson about complaining, anyway. I guess I'll have to save it for when we're alone."

"You could give it up altogether," she suggested with a twinkle in her eye.

"Yah… I don't think I can manage that. But Betsy needs to understand that the exercises are the right thing for me, even if I complain." He smiled a little. "So we've learned something about my sister, and all it cost was a black eye for you."

Startled, Miriam's hand flew to her eye. "What do you mean? I don't have a black eye. It's just a lump on my forehead."

"Today it's a lump on your forehead. By tomorrow it will be swollen around your eye and turning a lovely purple color."

She stared at him, seeing his smile. "You're joking. You can't be serious."

"I might be teasing you, but I'm not fibbing. That big lump on your forehead is going to go down to a black eye and most likely a bruise on your cheek, too. Trust me. It's happened to me more than once."

Miriam put her hand over her eye again, trying to imagine what it was going to look like. It was easier to imagine how her brothers were going to tease her.

"You don't have to sound so happy about it," she informed him. "It could have been you, you know. If those handles had hit you in the eye…"

"But my therapist's helper protected me, isn't that

right?" He was smiling, and his eyes twinkled for a moment.

Then, slowly, his expression grew more serious. His hand closed on hers. "I'm sorry you got hurt. Sorry I wasn't the one who protected you."

Their gazes locked onto each other, and it seemed to Miriam that the world around them pulled away, leaving only the two of them in a private circle of their own. She could hear his breath moving in and out, feel the warmth of his hand, and her own breath caught.

She couldn't be the only one feeling this. She couldn't. How could it only be on her side?

Chapter Six

By Thursday morning, Miriam was dumbfounded at the results of her black eye, which had appeared on schedule just when Matt had predicted. Everyone she encountered seemed compelled to comment on it, either teasing or openly curious, so she was grateful to stay at home when she wasn't at the King house.

Not that staying home let her avoid comments. The older boys found it a subject for teasing and jokes, with Daniel, in particular, coming up with a new joke about every hour. Josh, having been there for her accident, was more protective, while Sammy was speechless for once. The twins were the most surprising—they took one look at her and burst into tears.

Even now, and she started off to work, she found two pairs of small arms twining around her waist. Exchanging amused glances with Mammi, she bent and kissed one blond head and then the other one.

"I'm off to work, but I promise to be careful today. No more accidents, right?"

"Right," John Thomas and James answered in chorus.

"All right now, you two. Get off to your chores and let Miriam go. She'll be home to supper, and you'll see her then."

Mammi waved them off with her dish towel, and then came to give Miriam a hug of her own. "I wish…" She stopped and started over. "Are you sure this is the right job for you? Maybe Abel could find someone else."

"Are you trying to lose me my job?" she said lightly, aiming to chase away the concern on her mother's face. "I'm fine."

"This time," Mammi said, touching her cheek.

"Honestly, Mammi, after the way Abel scolded her, I'm quite sure Betsy isn't going to attempt anything else so foolish. I just wish I could find a way to help her." The children didn't know about Betsy's role in her accident, but she'd had to tell Mammi and Daad.

"Your tender heart will lead you into trouble one of these days," Mammi chided. "You have so much sympathy for everyone else, but you don't spare any for yourself."

Miriam blinked. "I don't need sympathy, Mammi. I'm doing what I was meant to do." She gave her mother a quick hug. "Now I'm off before it gets any hotter." She scurried out the back.

As she took off on the path along the pasture, the August day settled on her like a heavy blanket. It was going to be even hotter by the afternoon, but clouds were massing on the western horizon, promising storms before the day was over.

She touched the bruise on her face. It wasn't throbbing the way it had yesterday, at least, but she couldn't see that it looked any better. Maybe it was worth it, considering the way Matt had been pushing on his exercises since Tuesday. She'd thought he was cooperating earlier, but now he seemed determined to show her and Tim what he could do. Yesterday he'd gotten into the wheelchair with minimal help, though getting back into bed was more of a challenge.

She was happy with his progress, and Tim would be, as well. She just wished she knew how Matt himself felt about it.

Betsy wasn't around when Miriam got to the house, but Elizabeth greeted her with what was almost a smile. "Your face is looking better today, ain't so? I hope it doesn't hurt too much."

"I'm fine." She resisted the urge to put a shielding hand over her eye. It struck her suddenly that she ought to understand better Matt's reaction to his damaged face. It wasn't vanity, she thought. The idea that people were staring at you was enough to make her stomach twist anyway.

Elizabeth nodded, but she looked doubtful. "Is there anything you want help with today?"

Miriam hesitated. "Not really, but I would like to get Matthew out here to the table for lunch. What do you think?"

Elizabeth's faded hazel eyes filled with tears. "Ach, Miriam, that would be wonderful gut. Do you think we can?"

"We'll give it a strong try." She smiled, relieved at

Elizabeth's reaction. Elizabeth had said *we*. She had come a long way since the first day Miriam was here, and that was fine to see.

When she went into Matt's room, he took one look at her black eye and winced, turning his face away.

"No need for you to be embarrassed," she said lightly. "I'm the one who has to answer all the questions and deal with the smart remarks. I've decided that a black eye brings out the joker in people."

He seemed to force himself to look at her. "Sorry. I wish I'd been wrong about it. What kind of jokes?"

She shrugged as she prepared the exercise apparatus for use. "Did I have a fight with the broom when I was sweeping? Did I walk into the barn door? Nothing really very clever, but everybody has to make a comment."

"Maybe that's because they know it's not permanent. Not like this." He gestured toward the scarred side of his face.

Miriam paused before handing him the weights he was working with today. "You probably won't believe it, but I really don't see it any longer. I don't think your family does, either."

"You're right. I don't believe it." He grabbed the weights from her and began to lift them, frowning.

"That's too bad." She corrected his arm position. "That you don't believe it, I mean. But there's one thing this has taught me—that I'm just as self-conscious about my looks as the next person. I keep wanting to hide it."

"You're not going to fight with me today, are you?"

His lips twitched in a smile. "Why are you being so understanding?"

"I'm not." She smiled in return, relieved that at least he could talk about his scarring. "I'm saving arguing for something bigger. Let's try the side lifts now."

He didn't pursue the topic, and she was glad. She had a feeling he was going to battle the idea of going out to the kitchen for lunch. What would be the best approach? Reminding him that Tim had instructed him to? Pointing out that his family wanted it? Or as a last result, suggesting it was selfish of him to insist on having lunch brought to him?

She still hadn't decided by the time they had finished the exercises. Well, maybe she should…

Matt caught her hand as he gave her the exercise bands he'd been using. "Okay, you may as well tell me. Do you think I don't know when you're plotting something? What is it this time? Some new way of making me miserable?"

"Are you talking about your body or your disposition?" She kept her voice light, reminding herself that part of her job involved touching him. It was no different just because he'd been the one to initiate that handclasp.

"Both," he said shortly. "They go together, ain't so?"

Matt had a way of going right to the heart of the matter, and it felt as if he was always a step ahead of her. Maybe it was just impossible to surprise someone who'd known you since childhood.

She moved the wheelchair into position next to the bed, and he glared at it. "Not this again."

"Yah, this. You're doing it really well now. Don't you like doing something you've mastered?"

"You make me sound like a trained animal," he muttered, but he maneuvered into position, swinging his legs off the bed. "Do I get a treat when I do it?"

"Of course." She couldn't keep from smiling at that. He might not consider it a treat, but he should.

Without asking anything more, he moved into the process, going through each step Tim had impressed upon them. When she reached to help him, he shook his head. "I'll do it myself."

For an instant she felt panic. Was she pushing him too far, too fast? Before she came up with an answer, he'd done it, and he wheeled himself a few feet from the bed. He was trying to show nothing, but she could read the satisfaction in his eyes.

"Wonderful gut!" She felt like clapping, but he probably wouldn't appreciate that.

He grimaced, yet she knew better. "So, what is my treat?"

"You get to go out to the kitchen and have lunch with the family."

She grasped the handles of the wheelchair and held her breath for the argument.

He waited a moment too long before he answered. "What if I don't want to go?"

She started pushing. "You do want lunch, don't you?"

Grabbing the wheels, he stopped the chair abruptly, twisting his head to look at her. She smiled at him, but she knew she must look both scared and hopeful.

She watched the stubbornness drain out of him, and finally he nodded. "Okay. Let's try it."

With a singing heart, Miriam pushed the chair toward the kitchen.

Matt discovered he was holding his breath as he was propelled into the kitchen. Why was he so ferhoodled about something so ordinary? Foolish—that's what it was. Just because he hadn't been out here for a meal since he came home from the hospital...

The rest of the family was already seated at the table. Daad, beaming, jumped up to pull a chair away to make room for the wheelchair, and Mammi smiled with tears in her eyes. Betsy managed to look both sulky and glad at the same time, which was quite a trick. Miriam could be right about her.

Miriam's brother Joshua, grinning, helped her move the wheelchair into position. Matt caught him giving his sister a wink. Looked like he considered this an accomplishment. Did everyone in the community have an opinion about what he should or shouldn't be doing?

"Have some potpie." Miriam passed him the yellow earthenware bowl Mammi always used for chicken potpie, and other bowls began circulating around the table.

They must have had silent prayer before he got out here, he realized. Had his mother been praying for this moment? Maybe so, because right now she looked as if someone had given her a present. The least he could do was try to behave normally and act as if he were glad.

That meant joining in the conversation. Josh was asking Daad about the tomato baskets for market. For just an instant, Matt imagined it was David asking the question. David, who wasn't ever going to be here again. Angry at himself, he forced himself to focus.

"Good crop of tomatoes this year, Daad?"

His father looked enormously pleased at his asking the simple question. "Yah, yah, some nice big slicing ones, as you can see." He nodded toward the plate filled with rich red slices of beefsteak tomatoes.

"The sauce tomatoes are gut, too," Josh volunteered. "My mamm's been making quarts and quarts of sauce this week. Ask Miriam." He grinned. "She goes home from here and jumps right into hauling canning jars around. The kitchen is like a hot bath."

"We haven't even started." Mammi looked stricken, as if she'd been failing in her duties.

"I'm sure you have plenty left from last year," Miriam intervened. "Didn't I see them on the shelves when I went down in the basement?"

The upset look faded from his mother's face at the reminder. "Ach, yah, that's true. Still…" She seemed to be mentally counting out quarts of tomato sauce and juice.

"We don't need any more," Betsy said quickly, clutching at Miriam's comment, probably because she saw herself dragged into the canning operation Mamm usually had going this time of year.

Matt decided it was time to switch off the subject. "What did you end up putting in the north field, Daad?"

"Just letting it lie fallow this year. I'm thinking it might be good for cabbages. You ought to take a look at it. Maybe..." He let that trail off, maybe not sure what Matt's reaction should be.

As for him, all he could do was cringe inside at the thought of venturing even that far. Why did folks keep pushing him? He couldn't be any use to Daad even if he did go look at the field. Just because he let Miriam bulldoze him into coming out for lunch didn't mean he wanted to go anywhere else.

Before he could find a nice way of saying he didn't want to, Josh had already jumped on the idea. "We could easily put a ramp up to the porch. Remember, Miriam, when we built the ramp for Grossdaadi? It worked fine to get a wheelchair outside."

"That's an idea," Daad said, and Matt could see his enthusiasm building.

"I don't think I need it," he said firmly. "Besides, you've got plenty to do without building ramps."

Josh didn't seem to catch the message of his frown. "No problem," he said lightly. "I can get Daniel and Sammy to come over one evening and do it."

"It's none of your business." Betsy butted in with a glare at Miriam, as if this conversation was her fault. "It'd be too much for Matt."

"Betsy." Daad didn't have to say more than her name to shut her up. She was already in trouble over Miriam's injury.

Matt would have to do something about Betsy. Somehow he'd have to convince her that...well, he didn't know. Maybe Miriam would have some idea how he could get her to let go of her determination to protect him.

"Anyway, it would be too hard for anyone to push me that far over rough ground." He hoped he said it with enough finality that they'd get the message.

"Miriam, what about that battery-powered scooter you were telling us about in one of your letters?" Josh asked. "You said that guy you worked with could get all over the place using it."

"I… I didn't realize I'd mentioned it."

There it was again, Matt realized. That sense of something uncomfortable, even painful, about Miriam's time in Ohio. What had happened to her out there?

"It would have to run off the electric, wouldn't it?" His father was frowning at the idea.

"That would be out of the question for us," Matt added quickly.

"The scooter is battery-powered."

Miriam wasn't looking at him when she spoke. Maybe she hadn't intended to bring this subject up at all until Joshua forced it. Why?

Daad looked interested. "But you must have to charge the batteries, ain't so?"

"Yah, but the…the family I worked with had figured out a way to charge the battery using the milk cooler. In fact, the family bought two batteries for the scooter so one could be charging while the other was in use."

"Do you know where they got it, or what kind it was?" Daad had taken a piece of paper and a pencil from a kitchen drawer and was jotting down notes.

"I'm afraid I don't, but I expect Tim would know all about it, if you wanted to talk to him. Or I could call to find out."

Matt realized he had to stop all this before Daad spent a lot of money he couldn't afford on something that wasn't going to give him his legs back.

"I don't want a power scooter." He was trying to say it firmly, but it came out sounding loud and more angry than he'd intended.

Nobody said anything for a few moments, and he felt, without anyone saying anything, that they were disappointed in him. The weight of that disappointment was heavy on him.

"Sorry." Joshua's face grew red. "I just thought you might be interested."

Now he'd succeeded in embarrassing Joshua, who was only doing his best to help out. Daad's disappointment was obvious, and as for Miriam...

He couldn't mistake the look on Miriam's face. She was angry. In fact, she looked ready to tell him exactly what she thought of him for picking on her little brother. Her expression reminded him irresistibly of a moment on the schoolyard when she'd flown out after one of the older boys for hassling a smaller child. She'd been angry then, too.

When it came to defending someone who was smaller and weaker, quiet, gentle Miriam had had no fear. He'd try not to forget that again.

A rap on the screen door announced the arrival of Tim, breaking an uncomfortable silence. Miriam got up quickly, relieved to have an excuse to move, but Abel had already gone to the door and was greeting him.

"Komm, sit. You'll have a cup of coffee, yah?" Abel pulled up a chair.

"Well, since my client is still having lunch, I guess I will." Tim smiled impartially around the table. "Matt, I'm glad to see you out here for your lunch. That's a good sign."

Matt looked about to say something negative, but Elizabeth set coffee and a slice of apple pie in front of Tim. "Yah, very gut," she said, smiling at Matt with a look of pride. Whatever Matt had on the tip of his tongue, Miriam thought he swallowed it.

Tim murmured his thanks for the pie and coffee, taking a big bite of pie before he said anything, and then it was to praise the apple pie.

"My mammi makes wonderful gut pie," Betsy said, darting a look at her father as if to be sure he noticed her being polite.

But Abel had his mind on something else. "You would say that Matt is making gut progress, ain't so?"

Tim nodded, and Miriam had a feeling he was trying to decide how much to say. He wouldn't want to make any predictions about recovery. She was certain of that. "Progress is always good." Tim hesitated. "Injuries like Matt's can take a long time to heal."

"Very long," Matt added. "Months."

"Sure, but now the bones have come together well enough that we can really work on rehabilitation. You should start to see faster progress, even if it seems like a long time to you." Tim spoke with the air of one who had heard all the complaints his clients could come up with. "Trust me."

He looked at Matt as if expecting some response, but Matt just set his jaw stubbornly. Miriam didn't have any trouble interpreting that look. If they couldn't make him the way he was before, he wasn't interested. If only she had something encouraging to say...

But Tim took a last taste of pie, said thanks again, and stood up. "Miriam and I need to talk about the upcoming exercises, so we may as well do it first, while Matt finishes lunch." He nodded to the door. "Let's take a little walk to help me digest that wonderful pie."

Miriam followed him outside, feeling Matt's eyes on her as she went. Sooner or later, he'd be wanting to know what they'd talked about.

Tim took a deep breath as they headed toward the barn. "I've been stuck inside all day, and I'm glad to smell some fresh air for a change. And get away from town for a bit." He glanced sideways at her. "Good work on getting Matthew out of that room to eat lunch with his family. I want to hear about it. But first, tell me how you got that black eye."

She'd known that would be coming. "It was nothing. I yanked on the overhead cords, and they came down suddenly and hit my forehead. That's all."

He gave her a skeptical look. "You're sure that's all you want to say about it?"

"I'm sure," she said firmly.

Tim's concern wasn't allayed. "If it was Matt..."

"Oh, no. He had nothing to do with it. Really."

He nodded, accepting it but not fully convinced, she thought.

"Okay, if you say so. Anyway, getting him out with other people is great. Did he give you a fight about it?"

"Not as much as I expected. But then over lunch, someone mentioned taking him outside, and he had all sorts of objections to that." She sighed. "I know I shouldn't push too hard, but if I don't, he wouldn't move at all."

"Not unusual," Tim said. "The longer a patient has been down, the harder it seems to get him to tackle anything different. Their room becomes a refuge, and they're leery of what will happen if they go out. Of course, all that time in a hospital bed would discourage anyone."

"Especially someone who's so used to being active and working outside." She gave a fleeting thought to Matt the way he used to be. "I know his mood isn't really your job..."

"But it is." Tim stopped, turning to face her and looking steadily into her eyes as if to impress his words upon her. "A lot of recovery is mental and emotional. If that holds the patient back, then it's our business."

"Ours?" She wasn't sure she liked the sound of that.

He grinned. "You'd better face it, Miriam. He's not going to talk to me about what's causing his attitude. But you've known him all your life, so I hear. If anyone can get him talking, it's you."

She shook her head, doubting it. "Maybe his parents would be better."

"Sometimes that works, but not in this case. Their feelings must be awfully close to the surface after losing their younger boy. It might cause more harm than good." He gave her a sympathetic look. "I know you don't want to, but unless you know someone else he's close to, it comes down to you."

A sense of helplessness swept over her. "I wouldn't know where to start."

Tim shrugged and started walking again. "His attitude could be due to any number of things. Maybe more than one. In this case…well, I read up on the accident. Terrible thing."

"Yah, it was." She'd grieved for David's lost life even though he wasn't part of her family. "David was such a fine, loving boy." She was afraid her emotions were near the surface, too.

"Any negative feeling can hamper recovery. Fear, loneliness, loss of confidence, grief, even guilt." He stopped again, studying her face. "All I know is, if you can get him to realize what it is and accept it, he'll be able to move forward."

And if not? She followed Tim, heading back, and she noticed something at one of the windows. The curtain fluttered as if it had just been moved. As if someone had been looking out, watching them.

Chapter Seven

Miriam was up and moving early, but she hadn't gained any wisdom during the night. She still had no idea how to get Matt talking about his feelings. What's more, she had to admit that she was almost afraid to try.

Thankful that she didn't have to help with the milking as she had when the boys were too young, Miriam hurried to the kitchen. Mamm was already cooking hot cereal and had eggs ready to go as soon as the milkers came in.

"Miriam, I just remembered… I saw Beth when I went to town yesterday. She says what about having a cousins' picnic on Saturday at her place? I told her I'd have you call her." She shook her head. "I don't know how I could have forgotten last night."

Miriam gave her mother a hug and took over the cereal. "Maybe it's because there are so many of us that we talk you silly."

"Ach, you know I love it. But it does get a bit noisy around the table, yah?"

"It does. Especially since Josh is talking so much. He's really become more outgoing, ain't so?"

Mammi nodded, getting a pitcher of milk from the gas refrigerator. "He's growing up. Feeling more sure of himself, too." She paused, turning to Miriam. "You should be free to go Saturday afternoon. You can't be working all the time."

"I'd love to go. I guess I have been concentrating pretty hard on Matt and his family."

"You need a break," Mamm said firmly, giving her a searching glance. "Is something worrying you about Matt? Or the others? If there's anything I can do, I will."

"I know, Mamm." After all, she'd learned how to care for her neighbors from her mother. "Not really worried so much as wondering how to do something the therapist wants."

"Didn't he show you how?"

She shook her head, smiling a little. "If he could, that would be easy."

Was it right to talk it over with Mamm? Surely it was, especially if her mother could help her see what to do.

"Tim says that Matt's attitude is holding him back from healing. He thinks it would help if I could get Matt to talk about it. But I don't know if I can. If I ask him directly, I know he'd just be angry."

"Yah, that's certain sure." Mammi's forehead wrinkled. "The only way I can see is to listen when he does want to talk." She hesitated, seeming troubled. "Are you sure…"

"What?" She lifted the pot from the burner, hearing voices coming across from the milking shed.

Her mother reached out to touch her cheek lightly. "I wouldn't want you to be hurt." The look she gave Miriam squeezed her heart.

"If it helps Matt…well, I guess I have to do it anyway. You always say that the job God puts in front of us is the one we must do. No matter what."

"I guess I do think that," Mammi said, her expression rueful. "But it's different when it's my child who might be hurt."

She had only time to exchange an understanding look with Mammi before the boys came in clamoring for breakfast, and the moment was over. But still, she felt comforted.

Since every option she could think of to get Matt talking was a dead end, Miriam decided the sensible thing was to focus elsewhere. She walked along the field, feeling the warmth of the morning sun already hinting at the heat coming later. That room of Matt's would be stifling by afternoon. Maybe she could persuade him to go out on the porch if there was a breeze.

She considered the likelihood of his agreeing. Just because she no longer saw the scarring on his face, that didn't mean he wasn't sensitive about it. If she promised to take him inside immediately should anyone come, maybe he'd go along with it. All she could do was try.

And keep on trying, she reminded herself. Working with Matt was certain sure not as easy as working with her aunt had been. And the answer to that was surely that God hadn't promised it would be easy…just that He would be with His servants.

To her pleasure, when she arrived, she found Matt in his wheelchair at the kitchen table, a mug of coffee in front of him.

"This is nice to see…" she began.

Betsy jumped in before she could finish. "I helped Matt come out." Her tone implied the words she didn't say… *We don't need you.*

Miriam just smiled at her. "That's great, Betsy. I'm so glad."

Betsy didn't look as if she believed that. Too bad, because it happened to be true. If everyone in contact with Matt started pulling in the same direction, they could surely do great things.

"Seems to me I deserve some credit. After all, coming out for meals was my idea." Matt smiled up at his mother as she refilled his coffee mug.

His idea? Miriam seemed to remember it differently, but she was too pleased and amused to say so.

"You'll have some coffee before you start working, ain't so?" Elizabeth was already pouring it, not waiting for an answer.

"Denke. Better to have the hot coffee now than later. It feels as if it's going to be a scorching day," she commented.

"That probably means that Mammi is going to bake bread, just to heat the kitchen up even more." Matt's teasing tone brought a smile to his mother's face.

"I don't see you rejecting the bread, ain't so?" She

patted his shoulder, and Miriam realized that for a few minutes she looked like her old self again.

Good job, she thought, watching Matt's face. It was the first time she'd heard him make any of the easy, laughing comments that usually flew around the kitchen whenever a family was gathered. Just that simple thing had lightened the atmosphere of the kitchen so that it seemed the heat didn't matter at all.

Elizabeth moved off, following Betsy toward the hall to tell her something, and Miriam took advantage of the moment.

"That was *gut*, teasing your *mamm* that way. You made her happy."

She thought at first that he was going to snap back at her, but he didn't. He frowned down at his hands on the table.

"David used to tease her a lot. He always knew how to make people smile."

She nodded, brushing away a tear even as she smiled. David had had a gift that way.

Matt set his mug down and turned the wheelchair away from the table. "If I can make her smile…" he paused, his voice husky "…well, it's the least I can do."

With a push of his hands, he set the chair rolling toward the hall. She got up quickly, her mind spinning even as the wheels turned.

What did Matt mean by that? *Yah*, it would help his mother if he did so, but why did he say it was the least he could do? She found herself questioning Matt's every comment, looking for what it meant. And not understanding it.

* * *

By the time they were finishing lunch, Matt felt as if he were melting in the wheelchair. And that was nothing compared to the way Daad and Josh looked, although Daad's weathered face didn't show much reaction. Joshua was redder than any apple, but he still managed to smile as Daad got up from the table.

Knowing it would do no good, Matt still had to try. "Daad, how about knocking off early today? This heat's bad for anyone to be working in." He wanted to add, *especially someone your age*, but Daad would explode at the suggestion that he couldn't keep up with what he used to do.

"Ach, we're used to it, ain't so, Josh?"

Poor Josh couldn't do anything but nod.

"You'll take the jug of water with you," Mamm said firmly. "Sit down in the shade every so often. We can't—" She stopped short, but Matt knew just what she would have said. *We can't lose you, too.*

Silence spread around the table, and he noticed Miriam take a quick look at him. She wouldn't see what he felt, because he'd learned how to keep his emotions hidden.

Miriam seemed to know him better than he'd ever have thought, but she couldn't know this. No one would know that he was eaten up with guilt inside for all that this family had lost. If he'd pulled over farther, if he'd seen the car earlier, if he'd been a bit smarter, a bit faster...

After a few more minutes at the table, Daad and Josh were gone. Mamm and Betsy were clattering dishes in the sink, while Miriam came to grasp the handles of the wheelchair.

"What about going out on the porch? It's shady now, and there's a breeze. It will be much cooler than inside."

He grasped the wheel before she could move him. "If anyone comes, you get me inside at once." His words were sharper than he'd intended, but maybe it was just as well. Miriam had to understand there were things he wouldn't do.

"If that's what you want." She pulled the wheelchair away from the table and moved him toward the screen door. In response to a gesture from Mammi, Betsy hurried to hold it open.

"Denke, Betsy." Miriam's voice was as soft and peaceable as usual, but Betsy only glared.

Daad had insisted that Betsy apologize to Miriam, but maybe he should have left it alone. Saying the words hadn't changed what was in Betsy's heart, it seemed. And Matt guessed Miriam was willing to forget it.

Miriam settled his chair in a shaded spot where a breeze from the west provided intermittent cooling, and then she drew another chair over to sit next to him.

"You can digest your meal where it's slightly cooler before we start on your afternoon exercises." Miriam raised her face as the breeze came again, letting it lift strands of silky hair.

"Too bad we couldn't convince Daad to do the same." He watched Daad and Joshua walk across the field, Josh carrying a coil of wire and a handful of tools. "Mending fence is hot work."

He brooded, looking after them, then darted a glance at Miriam. "Aren't you going to try convincing me that I'm still of some use to the family?" Bitterness was acrid in his mouth.

She shook her head. "Maybe you're not, the way you mean. Not right now. But there's more to being part of a family than the labor you provide."

"Or don't provide," he said flatly. "Daad needs help to keep the farm going, and there's not a single thing I can do." He discovered he actually wanted her to argue with him, just for the doubtful pleasure of proving her wrong.

"Maybe not now, but nobody expects you to until you're healed."

"I expect it," he snapped. "Now is when Daad needs me. And don't bother talking to me about your brother. Josh is a gut boy, but Daad needs his own son. David is gone, and I'm useless."

He looked at her to find her studying his face as if trying to read his thoughts. That steady gaze made him feel uneasy. Was she thinking he sounded like a spoiled child? He did, of course, but the guilt that gnawed at him had that effect.

When she didn't speak, his discomfort grew. "Well? Aren't you going to convince me that one day I'll be back the way I was before?"

"I can't, because I don't know it. Nobody does." Her expression was serious, as if everything he said deserved attention. "I just know that if you do your therapy, you'll be better than you are now. If you don't, you won't."

"So you and Tim and the doctors say, but it doesn't help." He nursed his bitterness, letting it grow. "If someone had taken the keys away before that kid got into the car, I wouldn't be here. If I'd swerved sooner, or pulled off the road so he could pass…"

"You can't prevent an accident with wishful thinking." Miriam seemed to be holding on to her quiet tone with an effort. "It was an accident. No one intended it to happen."

"Is that supposed to make me feel better?" he snapped.

Miriam stood up, startling him.

"Leaving me?" He couldn't blame her if she did, and it would be a relief not to have to live up to her expectations. He was beginning to wish he'd never made that promise.

"I'll go and get the equipment ready for your exercises. Maybe that will put you in a better mood."

He looked up, ready to argue, but she'd already gone into the house before he could find a word. He heard her say something to Betsy, heard a snarled response from his sister.

"I thought you might like to work through the exercise routine with your brother," Miriam said patiently. "Then you could help him with it when I'm not here."

"Why? He doesn't want to waste time on those stupid exercises. He told me so. Why can't you leave him alone?"

"Because I want him to get better, and that's the only way to do it." Miriam's voice rang out clearly as he turned toward the screen door.

"That's what you say."

If Daad could hear Betsy, she'd be in for another punishment. And if he sat here and did nothing, he'd be helping her get into trouble.

With a wave of shame, he realized that Betsy wasn't nearly as rude to Miriam as he had been. He grabbed the wheels and shoved himself toward the door, reaching it in time to see the two of them staring at each other.

"That's enough, Betsy. Do what Miriam says."

She spun toward him, startled. "But I thought you didn't want to do those stupid exercises. That's what you said."

He had to force the words out, and they almost choked him. "Yah, I said it. But I was wrong."

Well, he had been. Not because he had much hope for the exercises, but because he'd agreed to them. Still, he hated to admit his fault with Miriam standing there staring at him.

By Saturday afternoon, showers had chased some of the oppressive heat away. As Miriam walked along the path into the woods with her cousins, laden down with picnic baskets and a jug of lemonade, she felt her spirits lift.

"I feel as if I'm about eight years old again," Miriam said. She smiled as Beth, ahead of her, glanced back over her shoulder.

"You don't look much older," Beth said.

"Wait a minute." Lyddy poked Miriam from behind.

"I'm younger than Miriam by three whole months, ain't so?"

"Maybe she thinks your approaching marriage makes you look older," Miriam teased.

"Well, I feel eight, too. And the raspberry bramble that just caught my apron is probably the same one that did back then."

"More probably its great-great-granddaughter." Miriam felt like skipping along the path downhill to the stream, but most likely she'd end up flat on her face if she did. There seemed to be a lot more tree roots snaking across the path than there used to be when they were children.

Still, it felt safe and familiar, walking down to the creek in the heat of an August day, eager to plunge her feet into the cool water. And there it was, rippling over the rocks that it had smoothed and flattened over years and years, since long before any of them were born.

"Here we are," Beth said as she stepped onto the oblong flat rock that jutted into the creek, causing the water to swirl around it. This had always been their picnic spot...the place where they'd sit and eat jelly sandwiches and whoopie pies, then take their shoes off and dangle their feet in the water.

Miriam paused to set the jug of lemonade she carried in the small pool created by the rock, wiggling the jug to be sure it wouldn't tip over. As soon as she drew her hand away, a flurry of minnows swam around it as if thinking it a strange newcomer to their watery home.

When she rose, Lyddy was already spreading a blanket for them to sit on while Beth started to unpack the picnic basket. Tradition said they'd eat first, talking about what everyone had been doing and then wade in the creek, catching minnows and the occasional crayfish.

"What do you think, Miriam?" Beth held up a packet of sandwiches. "Ham salad or pickle and egg?"

"If there's no peanut butter and marshmallow crème," she said, mentioning a favorite gooey treat from childhood, "I'll have half of each."

Laughing a little, Beth doled out the sandwiches, and talk began to ripple back and forth, just like the water chuckling past. They knew each other so well, and yet they never ran out of things to talk about. Anyone would think they'd already said everything there was to say, but anyone would be wrong.

Eventually, after tales from Beth about the silly things that happened in the store she ran with her husband, and the latest funny thing her son had said, Lyddy turned to Miriam.

"Your turn," she said. "We really want to know how Matthew King is doing. Are you ready to throw up your hands yet? Or has he tried to kick you out?"

Miriam smiled, relaxing back on her elbows, her legs stretched out on the cool rock. "You ought to know I've never been one to give up," she said. "Although Matt does try my patience from time to time."

"From what I remember about Matt, it would be more than just trying," Lyddy said, wrapping her arms around her knees. "He's one who always got his own way, or he'd know the reason why."

"Well, he usually thought he was right about whatever it was, and as often as not, he was right," Beth pointed out.

"He'd do even better if he set all that determination toward getting well, but he is doing better. This week we got him to join the family for meals, and yesterday he actually sat out on the porch for a gut long time. He was cross, but he did it."

"That's wonderful gut," Lyddy exclaimed. "From what I'd heard, I thought he'd never be out of the bed again."

But Beth was studying Miriam's expression. "What's wrong? That should make you happy, ain't so?"

"It does," she protested. "Well, mostly."

"Then what?" Lyddy turned from watching the minnows flitting around in circles.

"Healing is more than just physical." Miriam struggled for the words to explain the thing she knew but had trouble rationalizing. "It's…being well inside yourself. Not arguing with God about it, but accepting and moving on."

"It's a lot to accept," Beth said softly. "David…well, everyone loved David. And Matt was driving."

Miriam nodded, a lump forming in her throat. "Grief is natural, but I think Matt actually blames himself for the accident. He won't listen to anyone telling him otherwise."

"Like you?" Lyddy clasped her hand for a moment.

"Maybe I shouldn't have pushed, but it just seemed so wrong to me." She wasn't sure whether she was trying to justify it to them or to herself. "An accident is an accident. It's something nobody can predict is going to happen. If you could, you'd prevent it. Nothing he could have done would have made any difference. I'm sure of that."

She could hear the passion in her voice and knew she was giving away her feelings with every word. It couldn't be helped, and at least she was saying it to Beth and Lyddy, knowing they would understand and not tell anyone.

Lyddy straightened, shoving her feet out in front of her as if she intended to jump up and do something about it. "But that's ferhoodled. The police blamed it entirely on the driver. That boy had been drinking, and he was driving too fast. My daad heard one of the policemen say that if it hadn't happened there, it would have been somewhere else."

"It's no good telling Matthew that. He persists in thinking he could have prevented it. It's tormenting him, and I really believe it's keeping him from getting well."

"Yah." Beth's voice was soft. "It's sort of like you, blaming yourself for what happened with that boy you took care of."

Miriam could only stare at her in disbelief. Beth—gentle, understanding Beth—couldn't be saying such a thing. "I'm… I'm not. And anyway, it's not the same thing at all."

"Isn't it?" Beth exchanged glances with Lyddy, and she realized they'd talked about it privately since the last time she saw them. "You had no idea what was happening with that boy, so how could you have prevented it?"

"It was my job to understand," she said stubbornly. "You can't compare the two things."

"Matt probably feels it was his job to keep David safe, but he couldn't," Beth said.

Lyddy clasped her right hand again, and Beth took her left. They sat there, linked, not speaking. Not doing anything but letting the words sink in.

Beth was mistaken, she told herself firmly. She might have wonderful insight into other people, but this time she was wrong.

A small voice spoke in the back of her mind. *What if she isn't wrong? What if you're caught up in futilely replaying the past, just like Matt is?*

She wanted to believe Beth was mistaken, but the more she thought of it, the more it wondered her. If what Beth said was true, what could she do about it?

If she couldn't heal herself, how could she hope to heal anyone else?

Chapter Eight

By Monday, Miriam was eager to dismiss all her questions and get back to work. Whatever her own problems, they couldn't keep her from doing her best for Matt.

Sunday had been off-Sunday, when worship wasn't held in their church district. Families either got together to enjoy one another's company or went to another district to worship. In their case, they'd entertained her mother's side of the family. Much as she loved them, it had been stressful.

Mammi was the youngest by far of her family, and with five older sisters to host, she had spent the afternoon mediating the inevitable spats they had whenever they were all together. Miriam had never been able to understand why they couldn't just enjoy being together, but when she'd said that to Mammi once, her mother had laughed and said the sisters *were* enjoying themselves. Squabbling was their means of conversation.

Maybe so, but it wasn't so pleasant for the onlooker.

And it wasn't much better when they united, only to wonder audibly why Miriam wasn't married yet.

After all that, Miriam gave her mother an extra-warm hug when she left for the King place on Monday morning. She probably needed it.

Miriam arrived to find that Elizabeth had put Matt and Betsy to work snapping beans at the kitchen table. Before she could comment, he'd pushed the wheelchair back from the table.

"Sorry, Betsy. You'll have to finish. Miriam's ready to put me to work."

"No fair," Betsy said, grinning. "You always have an excuse not to do kitchen work."

It was good to see Betsy smile after the way she'd been for the past few days. "I wouldn't let him get away with it if I were you," Miriam said, joining in the teasing. "Besides, he's exercising his fingers, ain't so?"

"Yah, for sure." Betsy put a strainer full of beans in his lap before he could protest.

Elizabeth handed Miriam a mug of tea fixed just the way she liked it. "You must have had a nice time with so many visitors yesterday," she said. "I noticed all the buggies pulled up by the barn."

She sounded a bit wistful, as if longing for the days when she had done so, and Miriam noticed that Matt's face tightened. He'd be blaming himself, she guessed, for his mother's lonely day.

"*Nice* wasn't the right word," she replied quickly. "It was my mother's family. My aunts argued all afternoon."

Elizabeth actually chuckled at that. "They always

did, especially Evelyn and Lizzie. What was it this time?"

"Aunt Evelyn's granddaughter had a new dress, and Aunt Lizzie thought the color made her look like an eggshell. Or maybe it was the other way around."

"It wouldn't matter to them, as long as they had something to fuss over," Elizabeth said.

"I'd rather have a quiet Sunday afternoon," Matt said abruptly. He pushed the strainer over to Betsy. "Anyway, Grossmammi was here, so we had company. Now isn't it time we were getting to work?"

"Yah, for sure." Miriam took another swallow of her tea and set the cup down. "Let's go."

No sooner had the door closed behind them than Matt turned on her. "I guess you think I should encourage my mother to invite every relation we have to come here and stare at me."

If he was looking for a fight, she wasn't going to indulge him. Besides, they both knew he'd only said it because he felt guilty. She'd begun to think that he took out his unhappiness on her because he certain sure didn't want to hurt his family.

"Your mother was glad just to have your grandmother here."

He shrugged, looking embarrassed. "Yah, she was." He seemed to struggle for a moment. "Sorry I snapped."

With no reply but a smile, she got out the weights Matt had begun working with. "Let's try the three-pound ones today." She handed them to him.

He grabbed them with more energy than he usually showed and started on the round of arm exercises. Maybe he'd work off the rest of his ill feelings that way.

Actually, she could understand how he felt about seeing people. After all, she'd experienced it herself with all the comments about her fading black eye the previous day. Every relative had wanted to hear the whole story until she was tired of telling it.

Still, Matt would have to get over that particular feeling if his family was ever to have a normal life again.

Trying to change the mood, she waved toward the wood carvings. "What would you think about setting up your wood-carving tools? You might like that better than snapping beans."

"Neither of them is much help to anyone." He met her eyes and shrugged. "I'll think about it."

The door opened just then to admit Betsy. "The beans are done. Did Matt tell you how I made him work out on Saturday?"

Miriam smiled at the enthusiasm in her voice. "No, he didn't. How about it, Matt? Did she push you?"

Matt surrendered the weights. "She did. I think she's been taking lessons from you and Tim."

Miriam liked seeing how Betsy blossomed at the compliment from her brother. "We were just talking about getting out his wood-carving equipment. What do you think?"

"Great. Remember, you promised to carve a cat for me when you had time. I know right where the tools are."

"I said I'd think about it," Matt protested, but more as a matter of form than anything serious.

"Don't bother thinking about it. Just do it," Betsy prompted. "That's what Grossmammi always says. Let's finish the exercises, and then Miriam can help me carry the table and equipment down from the attic."

"Sounds good to me." Miriam waited for another protest from Matt, but it didn't come. He actually looked enthused about it. For the first time, she felt optimistic about his recovery.

So it turned out that fifteen minutes later, having finished the first round of exercises, she and Betsy were toting a heavy table awkwardly down the attic steps.

"I know this is the right thing to do," Betsy said. "Once the wood-carving stuff is set up, he won't be able to resist. He…" She stopped while they made the turn at the bottom.

As they moved into the upstairs hallway, the sound of voices below came floating up. "Sounds like someone is here." Setting the table down, Miriam took a step toward the stairs, trying to determine who it was.

The voices became louder, and she and Betsy exchanged looks, recognizing the voices. Miriam felt her heart sink. "Liva Ann," she murmured.

"And her mother," Betsy added. "We'd better go down and help Mammi."

For once they were on the same side. They scrambled toward the steps, but even as they did, Miriam feared they were too late. That loud, cheerful voice sounded as if Liva Ann's mother was barreling right through Elizabeth.

"He'll love to see Liva Ann," she announced. "We'll go right in. Come on, Liva."

"Hurry," Betsy said. They scrambled down the stairs, but before they could reach the bottom they heard a shriek, a slamming door and then a crash.

Matt stared at the door, his hands clenched into fists, his stomach churning. She'd taken one look at him, and that had been enough to make her shriek. He heard Liva Ann muttering while her mother scolded, her voice fading as they apparently left the house.

He let out the breath he'd been holding. They were gone. How had they gotten in here?

The doorknob turned. He reached out and grabbed the nearest hard object…the flashlight that lay on the bedside stand. The door opened a crack and Miriam's voice floated through.

"I'm coming in. Don't throw anything."

The door swung open. Miriam came inside, her feet crunching on broken glass. She looked down and stepped clear of the remains of the canning jar he'd thrown. The daisies it had contained were scattered across the broken glass.

If Miriam said one word—

She turned back toward the hall. "Betsy, hand me the broom and dustpan, please."

Betsy apparently did, because a moment later Miriam was back, closing the door and beginning to sweep up the glass without comment.

For some reason, even her silence infuriated him. "If you were part of that, you'd better have a bigger dustpan."

She paused, looking at him. "Don't be foolish. You know I wasn't. Betsy and I were carrying a table down from the attic. And don't blame your mother, either. Dora Miller simply charged past her as if she weren't even there."

"Sorry," he muttered.

"Those were the daisies Betsy picked for you." She was still scolding. "You'd best tell her you're sorry."

His annoyance flared like a fire with dry kindling. "If someone screamed at the sight of you, you might throw something, too. At least I waited until she shut the door."

"Liva Ann? Yah, we could hear the screech from upstairs."

"I didn't have time to turn away." He glared at her, but Miriam seemed unaffected. "Liva Ann got the full effect of this." He smacked his palm against his scarred cheek.

Miriam kept on sweeping. "She doesn't seem to have much self-control, does she? But she's pretty young. She'll probably be better when she's older. Look at her mother."

"I don't want to look at her mother," he said, exasperated. "What does she have to do with it?"

"I'm just saying that she wouldn't scream. When Liva Ann is a little more mature…"

"I don't intend to wait until Liva Ann is more mature. Why are we talking about it?"

Miriam shrugged. "I was just pointing out that she'll probably have her mother's nerve when she's older. If you're going to marry her..."

"I'm not. I'll be happy not to see either of them ever again. If they come back, I'll throw something heavier than a canning jar full of daisies."

She stared at him for a moment, and a smile tugged at her lips. "I take it you're not heartbroken. You're just mad."

"Wouldn't you be?"

Miriam bent to sweep the glass into the dustpan. "If I loved somebody, it would be painful."

"You're trying to make me admit that I didn't love her." He rolled the wheelchair closer and took the dust-pan while she stood up.

"Well, you didn't, did you?" Her smile was more definite now.

He tried to hang on to his annoyance. He couldn't. To his astonishment, he discovered he wanted to laugh.

"I guess not." He chuckled. "But that was a spectacular way of finding out. That screech she let out..."

He wrapped his fingers around her wrist, feeling her pulse thud against his skin. He couldn't seem to find anything more to say, but he didn't want to let go.

Someone opened the door cautiously, and he pushed the chair back to empty the dustpan. Betsy looked around the edge of the door, and his mother appeared beyond her, both of them looking apprehensive.

"Everything all right?" Betsy's eyes were wide.

"Yah, it's over," he admitted. "Just watch for any glass."

"I think I got it all," Miriam said, not looking at him. She turned to Betsy. "Maybe we should get that table we left on the stairs."

In a moment she was gone, and he was left wondering what she was really thinking.

Mammi patted his hand. "Ach, I'm sorry. That woman—" She fought to control herself. "She just pushed right past me like I wasn't there. I'm sorry. I should have stopped her."

"Don't be sorry." He clasped her hand. "Maybe it was for the best. At least they won't come around anymore."

"But you...she hurt you."

He shook his head slowly. "Actually, it didn't hurt. It just made me mad. Miriam said that meant I never loved her at all."

Mamm actually smiled. "I never did think Liva Ann was the right girl for you. Maybe it's for the best."

"She can go back to her rumspringa parties and flirt with the boys," he said, realizing that prospect didn't bother him in the least.

"Who's going to rumspringa parties?" Betsy came in, walking backward and carrying one end of the chair.

"Liva, I hope," he said. "She should find some nice boy to court her."

"As long as it's not you," Betsy declared. "She's too silly for you."

Miriam had appeared with the other end of the table, and they set it against the side wall next to the bookcase.

He looked from one face to another. "It sounds as if all of you have the same idea. You must be right." He rolled his chair toward the table. "This will be perfect. Did you find the boxes with the tools?"

"I'll get them," Miriam said, moving quickly.

He was about to say that Betsy could do it, but Miriam was already gone. Was it his imagination, or was she trying to stay away from him?

Maybe she hadn't liked it when he'd grasped her wrist. He hadn't meant to offend her. It was just a friendly touch. He hadn't meant anything by it. Had he?

Miriam could only be thankful that Tim would be coming in the afternoon. That way, she didn't have to be alone with Matt, something too dangerous for her self-control. Dealing with this morning's events had been enough for one day.

Conversation bounced around the table during lunch as everyone seemed to react cheerfully to the fact that Liva Ann was out of their lives. And mostly, it seemed, that Matt didn't care a bit about losing her.

The lively chatter proved to be a useful distraction for Miriam from those moments when Matt's hand had encircled her wrist. His touch had gone right to her heart. Her breath had caught in her throat. Everything she thought she knew about herself turned upside down, and it still hadn't righted itself. All she could do was hope that he hadn't realized what was happening to her.

Miriam heard her name and surfaced, hoping no one realized she hadn't been listening. Josh was speaking, and it seemed he'd asked her a question. She hadn't the faintest idea what that question had been.

"There comes Tim," he said, glancing toward the window that overlooked the lane. "I'll ask him. He'll know exactly how the ramp should be built."

"You don't need to." Matt sounded as if he was trying to stop a flood with his bare hands. "I don't want…"

He stopped, because no one was paying attention to him. Josh was getting up from the table and carrying his dishes to the sink. In a moment, Abel had followed him.

"I can stop by the lumberyard and get the planks you need," Abel said. "It's wonderful kind of you and your brothers."

"There's nothing the boys enjoy more than making a big mess building something," Josh said.

Miriam had caught up with the conversation by now. Josh was determined to build a ramp off the porch for Matt, and his enthusiasm had pulled his brothers along on the project.

Josh grinned, turning from the sink. "Daad said he was sure he had enough planks for it. I'll check with him and bring them over next time."

Matt might as well save his breath, because it wouldn't change Josh's enthusiasm. Besides, she could see that Abel was just as eager. There'd be a ramp off the back porch before many days had passed.

Good. Matt would soon have no excuse not to join the world again.

Tim's van had pulled up by the porch, and he was calling for someone to give him a hand. Josh hurried out, followed by Abel. In another moment, Betsy had scurried after them.

Clattering and banging came floating in from outside. Miriam decided that whatever they were doing, they had enough help, so she finished clearing the table. With an expression that said he was giving in to curiosity, Matt wheeled himself to the door where he could see.

"What is that thing? Miriam?"

She came to look over his shoulders at the unloading that was in progress, but she'd already figured it out. "Parallel bars. So you can get upright again."

Miriam had turned to look at him when she spoke, and she couldn't miss the expression on his face.

"I don't want to use them," he muttered, and she didn't know if his words were born of fear of trying it or just plain stubbornness.

Deciding there was no comment she could make that would help, she ignored him, clattering the dishes to sound as if she were busy.

Something thudded onto the back porch, and then Betsy opened the door and held it wide. "Okay?" she called, probably to Tim.

"Right." Tim sounded cheerful. "Easy does it. We'll have to decide on the best place to put it."

Tim and Josh appeared, handling the set of bars between them. Miriam heard a sharp intake of breath beside her.

He was afraid, Miriam realized. Afraid of trying something new. Afraid of failing.

"You don't have to try it until you're ready," she said quickly. "I don't think Tim will push you on it."

"Good." Matt sounded as stubborn as ever. "Because I'm not ready." He folded his arms across his chest in a sign of conviction, but Miriam noticed how tightly clenched his fists were.

Meantime they had wrangled the apparatus into the kitchen and set it down for a consultation about where it might go. Aside from not being in the kitchen, Elizabeth didn't seem to mind where it was, and they eventually decided it could go next to the wall in Matt's room.

At that point, Miriam joined them, and when Abel and Josh hurried off to get some tools, taking Betsy with them, Miriam had a chance to tell Tim what was troubling her.

"Don't you think this is pushing him too fast?" She gestured toward the bars. "He doesn't feel he's ready."

"I know." Tim lowered his voice, stepping closer to her. "We'll move slowly, of course. Remember when we talked about the things that hold him back? I realized that maybe holding out a goal in front of him might have the opposite effect. Don't you think?"

Miriam hesitated for a moment, and then she realized what was happening to her. She had become too involved with Matt, and she cared too much. Her own emotions were getting in the way of what was best for him.

Forcing a smile, she nodded. "I'm sure you're right."

Tim studied her face carefully, probably knowing something was wrong. She waited for him to tax her with being too involved, but he didn't.

"Don't worry. We'll coax him into it, one baby step at a time. Remember, we can't guarantee anything, but we'll do everything possible to get the best result for our patient."

It was a reminder that she needed, she knew. Matt was a patient, and she had to see him that way. She couldn't let anything interfere.

For the rest of Tim's visit, she watched, along with Betsy, as he worked with Matt, demonstrating each new exercise slowly and carefully, showing Matt the brace that he hoped would stabilize his more seriously injured leg enough to allow Matt to stand.

They were getting into new territory this week, and she realized that Betsy was watching and listening to the description of each exercise just as carefully as she was. She felt a wave of gratitude for the girl. She'd come so far from her initial antagonism that she'd turned into a great help.

Miriam caught Betsy's eye as they each had a try with putting the brace on themselves to see how it felt. Betsy cared about her brother. That caring had been behind her attitude all along. It had just been misdirected at first. Now that she understood what was best for him, she'd be invaluable.

"Okay," Tim said at last. "Good work, Matt. Just your massage left to finish off the day, and none too soon, I'm sure you're thinking."

Matt gave a rueful smile. "You discovered a few muscles that I'd forgotten about, I'll say that for you."

Tim laughed, taking a mock punch at Matt's shoulder. "That's the way to look at it. Try some heat on it after your massage. You'll be ready to work on it again tomorrow."

Miriam walked out with Tim to hear his final instructions for the next few days. When he went off to give Josh a few tips about the ramp, she went back inside slowly. Her thoughts had been spinning so much that she felt as if she should curl up in a ball until they stopped, but there was no time for that. Her patient was waiting for his massage. Somehow she had to isolate her feelings and do it.

But when she walked back into Matt's room, she found that Betsy was already doing it. Startled, she paused. Before she could say anything, Matt spoke.

"Betsy can take care of this today. You're already late getting finished with all that's been going on. She'll even take care of the heat packs."

"I'm doing it right, ain't so?" Betsy said anxiously.

"Exactly right," Miriam said. Now her thoughts stopped spinning and landed with a thud. She had betrayed herself. Matt had recognized her rush of feelings when he'd touched her. He'd probably been embarrassed, unsure how to handle it. How to let her know that she was wrong.

So he was trying to let her down easy, holding her at arm's length. Telling her without a word that there could be nothing between them.

She couldn't control her blush, so she turned quickly away, trying to hide the color in her face as he had tried to hide his scar.

"I'll be glad to get off home." She walked steadily to the door. "I'll see you tomorrow."

Tomorrow, when she'd have figured out a way of controlling her feelings. Tomorrow, when she'd become adjusted to the fact that she was in love with Matthew, and he felt nothing in return. How was she going to deal with it?

Her future was just what it had always been, she assured herself as she walked quickly toward home. She would help other people heal. It was what she'd always wanted, and she would keep on doing it.

But now she knew that she could never heal herself.

Chapter Nine

Miriam and Betsy stood on either side of Matt, ready to help him stand. But Matt wasn't cooperating.

"We can wait until Tim arrives to do this one." Sitting in the wheelchair, which they'd pushed up to the bars, Matt planted his hands on the arms of his chair, as if he planned to stay there no matter what.

"You heard the message. Tim said to start without him, and he'd get here as soon as he could. That's right, isn't it, Betsy?"

Betsy nodded. She'd gone to the phone shanty when Tim didn't arrive at his usual Thursday time and found his message. "He said he was delayed at the appointment before ours. He didn't sound very happy about it."

"So, he's obviously late. We don't need to start with this exercise."

Miriam was more than a little disappointed. After what had been a shaky start to the week on Monday, she'd thought they were back to their friendly, patient-and-helper relationship again. Now why was he balking?

"You know why Tim wants you to do this after your warm-up stretches." Miriam said it as patiently as she could, but her exasperation probably seeped through. "Always do the hardest thing first." She found herself smiling as the memory popped up in her thoughts again. "According to my grossmammi, that's the rule for everything, not just exercises."

Betsy giggled. "Grandmothers have good advice for every subject, ain't so? Our grossmammi certain sure does." She nudged her brother. "You know she'd say the same thing."

"Maybe she would, but…"

"What's wrong? Can't you think of another excuse?" Betsy had gotten rather bossy with her big brother now that she thought it was her job to cheer him on.

Miriam decided she'd best intervene before it turned into a brother-sister battle.

"You may as well tell us what's really wrong. We're not giving up unless you give us a genuine reason." She grasped his arm firmly to help him up, and he jerked away.

Her face must have reflected the dismay she felt. She really had ruined things with her reaction to his unexpected touch on Monday. If Matt wouldn't let her touch him, she couldn't do her work. She'd have to quit.

"All right, I'll tell you." His lips quirked. "You'll drop me."

His sister swatted him. "Listen, the two of us are a match for you any day. Ain't so, Miriam?"

Her tension drained away, leaving a smile. It wasn't a good reason, but it was better than thinking what she had been.

"That's certain sure. Besides, we put the mats down. Even in the unlikely event that we let go of you, you'll have a soft landing."

"Judging by my sister's expression, it's not that unlikely." He extended his arm to Miriam. "Okay, I'll risk it if you'll keep an eye on Betsy."

"Nobody needs to keep an eye on me." Betsy grabbed his other arm. "Now quit stalling and get going."

Betsy might think she didn't need supervision, but Miriam watched to be sure her grip was correct. "You can use the bars to help as much as you want. You know you can count on your upper body strength."

"That's from all the hay bales he's tossed around," Betsy put in, bracing herself. "Ready?"

Miriam nodded. She had to hold his arm so closely that it pressed against her rib cage. Trying to block out every sensation, she counted down. "Three, two, one, lift."

In another moment he was standing, each hand clasping a bar. Cautiously, he straightened, putting more weight on his hands.

She watched his face, looking for any sign that he should be lowered back to the wheelchair. But he looked triumphant. Surprised at himself, but triumphant.

"Let go for a minute," he demanded.

Miriam exchanged looks with Betsy. He seemed to

be standing easily, and his grasp on the bars was firm. With a silent prayer, she nodded. Gradually she and Betsy loosened their grip, but Miriam kept her hands in position to grab him.

"I'm doing it." There was no mistaking the surprise and pride in his voice, and her heart sang.

"You definitely are. And that's about enough for the first time." She took his arm, just as the door opened.

"Wow." Tim grinned at the sight that met his eyes. "So this is what happens when I'm late. If I'm not careful, you won't need me at all."

"I'm not that far along." Matt eased himself back and let them help him sit down. "But it surely feels wonderful good to stand by myself."

Tim looked as happy as if it had been him. "Maybe I'll have to be late more often." His expression changed. "Scratch that. I shouldn't even joke about it. If it happens again with the same job, I'll…well, I don't know what I'll do."

"Problems?" Miriam asked, and Matt turned his chair slightly so he could see Tim's expression.

She could see the struggle on Tim's face. He was so frustrated that he looked ready to burst if he couldn't vent to someone.

"Okay, here it is without names. My last patient was a woman just home from the hospital after hip surgery. She and her husband had been instructed that she could not be left on her own yet." He grimaced. "When I got there, the husband was already in his car and ready to pull out of the driveway. I wanted to give him some instructions, but he sped away before I could. I guess he figured if I was there, he didn't need to be."

"The poor woman." Miriam's heart ached for her. "Is he the only person she can rely on?"

"Apparently, but you haven't heard half of it. The appointment was for one hour. I like to allow plenty of time to talk to the patient, especially the first visit. So the hour passed, and the husband wasn't back. I waited—I couldn't possibly leave her by herself."

"She must have felt terrible," Betsy said. She was obviously trying to imagine any of her family doing that, and failing.

"She kept urging me to leave, saying she'd be okay. But no way was I doing that. Anything could have happened to her. Forty-five minutes later, he showed up."

"I take it you gave him a lecture." Matt moved his chair back a little, facing Tim more completely.

"More than that. I told him his insurance wouldn't pay for the time he'd wasted, and he would be charged personally for it." He grinned. "That got him serious in a hurry. I won't have any more trouble with him, though his wife might." Looking better for having told the story, he patted Matt's shoulder. "You're one of the fortunate ones. You have people who love you to help."

Miriam froze for an instant. Tim didn't mean that the way it sounded, of course. But at that moment, she felt she'd like to hide.

A wave of energy powered Matt through the rest of his therapy session, so much so that Tim firmly removed the weights from his hands. "I can do more..." he began, but Tim shook his head.

"Enough. Just because you got on your own two feet doesn't mean you can tackle a mountain." He handed the weights to Miriam, and she stowed them on the bookshelf.

"It's nice to see though, yah?" Her warm smile seemed to congratulate Matt.

It also reminded him of the agreement they'd made about his therapy. He just might have to admit that Miriam had been right. After a session like this, he wasn't going to give up now.

"Come on, Tim. Admit it. I'm doing better than you thought I could." He swung the wheelchair around to follow Tim to the kitchen.

"I think you're looking for a compliment." Tim's usual smile widened. "You deserve one. You're doing great. So is your support team."

Matt glanced from Betsy to Miriam as he propelled himself into the kitchen. "That's certain sure. I couldn't do without them."

Betsy dashed away a tear and gave him a throttling hug. "You'd better not try."

Hugging her back, he looked at Miriam to find she'd turned away, but he couldn't miss the fact that she wiped her eyes, too. When she turned around, she had banished any sign of tears.

"Just don't get overconfident," she cautioned. "We don't want any accidents." For an instant her voice seemed to tremble on the words.

Or had he imagined it? No, there was something—

some emotion that she was hiding behind her gentle smile. He opened his mouth to ask when he was interrupted by a crash out on the back porch, followed by male laughter.

"What's going on out there?" He set the wheelchair in motion and got to the door first. Then reality set in, tempering his euphoria, when he had to wait for help to manage getting out the door.

Miriam pushed him outside. "This was going to be a surprise, but my brothers can't do anything quietly, ain't so?"

"We could have," Josh protested, "if we hadn't brought Sammy with us."

Ten-year-old Sammy turned to Matt with a grin, mischief lighting his freckled face. "It wasn't my fault. It was Daniel's. He was being so bossy that I told him to do it himself."

Daniel took a mock swipe at him, and he ducked away, laughing and still talking. "We're building you a ramp, Matt. Then you'll be able to get back to work."

Matt sensed Miriam freeze, as if she held her breath, waiting for an explosion from him.

But Sammy was just a kid. He joked with Matt the way he would with his older brothers, and it was impossible to be upset at anything he said. He reached out to tap Sammy's straw hat, tipping it over his eyes.

"Big talk," he said. "Let's see you do some work. I can probably still work harder than you, even in this chair."

Sammy just grinned with his usual good humor. He

reminded Matt so much of his own younger brother than his heart seemed to stop for a moment.

Someday would he be able to remember David without the flood of guilt and grief? He didn't think so. He guessed he would have to learn to live with it.

"Much as I'd like to join the work party, I've got another visit yet this afternoon." Tim rested his hand on Matt's shoulder. "Don't quit working. But don't try doing things on your own—that usually backfires."

Matt jerked his chin toward Miriam and his sister. "My guard dogs won't let me. You can count on that, ain't so?"

"Just try it," Betsy said, overhearing. "I'll land on you like a wagonload of hay bales."

"Good for you." Tim lifted his hand in goodbye as he strode off to his van, and Matt could almost see his mind shifting again to his next patient.

Miriam moved toward the door. "If you're going to stay here and supervise, I'll finish putting the exercise equipment away."

Matt nodded. "Don't let it worry you. Betsy will keep an eye on me."

"I'm sure of it." Laughing a little, she swung the screen door open.

Moving the chair to a better angle, Matthew could see the whole process. Obviously, the Stoltzfus boys had planned this carefully. They'd brought the parts of the ramp already assembled in the wagon that was pulled up on the grass, and with many hands available, they were putting it together. If it had been a barn raising, it couldn't have been better planned.

The ramp would go out from the porch at a gentle slope, then turn toward the lane and end just where buggies usually pulled up. He'd thought to stay for a few minutes, just to show he appreciated it, and found he couldn't pull himself away. Instead he watched it take shape and longed to have a hammer in his own hand.

"So, who was the designer?" he called. "Someone knew just how to go about this."

Daniel gave Josh a shove. "This guy. He talked to Amos Gaus about the one he made for his grandfather, and together they figured it out."

"Yah, but you did most of the carpentry, with Sammy's help."

Sammy blushed bright red, and the others laughed.

"If you can call it help to nearly nail his shoe to the plank…" Daniel teased.

Watching them work, Matt let his mind stray back to the day when he'd rejected the whole idea of a ramp. It struck him how selfish that had been. They were smiling, their voices light and joking. They were enjoying the job, not just because it was a change in the routine but because they were doing something good for someone else. He'd have let his own stubborn pride rob them of that pleasure and satisfaction.

It was as if he looked in a mirror, saw himself, and didn't like what he saw. He'd not just been selfish, he'd been self-pitying…hiding in his room when he should have been sharing his family's grief and helping them.

No more of that. Maybe it had been the elation of finding he could stand alone, but his plans had changed.

No more reluctance. He'd do everything he could to keep improving, even if it didn't get him where he'd like to be.

He owed it to all the people who cared about him. And he owed it to Miriam to tell her that their stupid agreement was over. When they'd made it, he'd been using it as a wedge to get Miriam out of his life. But Miriam was the one who'd helped him get this far. She deserved an apology.

Spinning the chair around, he headed for the door, and Betsy scurried after him. "What are you doing?"

"I need to talk to Miriam for a bit. Give me a hand with the door."

"I can get her—"

He shook his head. "I'd rather go in. I won't be long."

Obediently, Betsy pulled the door open and gave him a push over the slightly raised doorstep. "Just shout when you want to come back out."

He nodded, engrossed in what he was going to say.

Miriam was sliding the bars back against the wall. She obviously didn't hear him, and when she turned, she nearly tripped on the chair.

"Easy," he said, catching her arm. "You were making too much noise to hear me."

An outburst of hammering came from the porch, and she shook her head, smiling. "I couldn't compete with that. Do you need me?"

"Just to tell you something. About that agreement we made—remember that?"

For just an instant he thought she'd completely forgotten it. Then the puzzlement in her face faded. "I don't think our month is up yet, is it?"

"I don't need a month. You win."

"Are you sure you want to admit it?" she asked lightly, but pleasure brightened her eyes.

"Certain sure." He frowned a little. "Look, I know what Tim was thinking—that I'll never be back the way I was. But if I can't be that, at least I can be useful. I want you to stay. Unless you're tired of my complaining."

"Never that. As long as you need help, I'll stay." Something serious darkened her clear eyes for a moment. "Maybe it'll make up for things."

Her expression troubled him. "What do you need to make up for? You've done nothing but help people."

Miriam shook her head a little. "Nobody's that good. Nobody gets through without some scars, even if you can't see them, even if their intentions are good."

He studied her face, wishing he could see beyond the calm facade. He realized he still held her arm, and he let his hand slide gently down to her wrist, reluctant to let go. "I'm not convinced."

"It doesn't matter." She tried to shake it off. "I've had a failure or two. But if I can really help you, well, maybe it will make up for the ones I couldn't help."

He still wasn't satisfied, but he knew her well enough to understand she didn't want any more questions. So he nodded and squeezed her hand, then thought he probably shouldn't have.

"I'll do my part," he promised. He wanted to know

who it was Miriam thought she had failed, but unless she decided to confide in him, he'd never know.

Miriam moved away, a fixed smile on her face. This was too difficult—being with Matt every day, being close and hiding her feelings for him. It was easier when he snarled at her. She could take that. But when he smiled, when he expressed interest and concern, it was just too difficult.

But difficult or not, she had to manage. She was committed to help him for as long as he needed her.

A burst of laughter and cheering from outside was a welcome distraction. She hurried toward the door. They were calling for Matt.

"You're wanted out here. I'm afraid they're going to make you try it."

Matt wheeled himself across the kitchen. His movements were more sure every day, she realized. He'd probably be able to go in and out without help soon. She held the door and then followed him.

Her mamm and daad had shown up while they were inside, Mamm with a basket that probably contained food. She would think that any celebration ought to include food, and certain sure the boys were celebrating.

Matt must have seen her mother about when she did, and in what was probably a reflex, he turned his face away. So, he didn't mind her little brothers seeing him, but apparently a woman was different.

He surely couldn't think Mammi would shriek like Liva Ann. Miriam learned over the wheelchair and spoke in a low voice.

"Don't turn away from Mammi. If she can stay calm when the boys have been intent on mangling themselves, she's not going to be upset by a nice clean scar."

He glared at her for an instant. Then he nodded, and a smile tugged at his lips. "Guess you're right at that," he said, but it still seemed to take an effort for him to turn to face Mammi and speak to her.

A familiar pain cramped her heart. How could he think that a scar made him any less of a person? She longed to reach out and touch it soothingly, and the impulse was so strong that her palm actually tingled.

She pressed her hand firmly against her skirt, trying to chase away the feeling.

"It's finished," Sammy announced, standing at the entrance to the ramp. "Look!" He stepped aside, gesturing with a flourish, and making her wonder where he came upon that idea.

"You don't need to take the credit," Betsy teased, and in a moment they were shoving one another like the childhood playmates they'd always been.

"Behave yourselves," Mammi said impartially to both of them. She handed the basket to Elizabeth. "Just a little snack for everyone," she said.

"Ach, whoopie pies," Elizabeth exclaimed. "That's Abel's favorite. I'd best make sure some are put back for him before the young ones eat them all."

"He's coming now," Miriam said. "Don't let Matt start until his daad is here. I'll run and tell him."

She hurried out the lane, not so much because she thought they'd start without him, but because she could see his expression. He must have been out to the mailbox, judging by the envelopes in his hand. He stared at a paper open in front of him, and his face was so grim it startled her.

He didn't look up until she had almost reached him, and then had to blink before he seemed to register that she was there.

"Ach, I'm sorry, Miriam. I didn't notice..." He ran out of words, and the paper trembled in his hand.

Alarmed, she grasped his arm. "Are you all right? Was ist letz?"

He finally seemed to see everyone gathered around the ramp.

"The ramp is finished," she explained quickly. "They want you to come to see Matt try it. If you're all right..."

"Fine, I'm fine." He stuffed the paper into an envelope and put it underneath the copy of the Amish weekly paper. "It's about the trial. The boy who hit Matt and David." His voice shook as his hand had, and he took a breath. "It maybe will start as soon as next week."

Her thoughts made a leap to all that might mean to Abel and Elizabeth, indeed to all of them. But especially Matt.

"I must think about how to tell them." He clamped his lips on the words.

"Do you want me to...to make some excuse?" She gestured toward the house.

"No, no, I must go." He forced a smile and took a few steps forward before glancing at her. "Don't say anything to Matt."

"No, for sure I won't."

"Gut." He gave a short nod and then headed for the porch.

Miriam hurried along behind him, trying to wrap her thoughts around what this might mean. At the very least it would upset everyone. And Matt...

Matt hadn't come to terms with what happened. Maybe he never would. What was this going to do to his progress, which had seemed so bright just a moment ago?

Chapter Ten

By Friday morning, Miriam realized she had to talk to someone about the trial or burst. She'd spent a wakeful night, worrying, praying, and worrying and praying over and over.

Daad and the boys didn't seem to notice anything. They were still talking about how much fun it had been to build the ramp and watch Matthew use it.

"He can go anywhere now, can't he, Miriam?" John Thomas, the bolder of the twins, appealed to her.

James leaned over to whisper in his ear, and a silent conversation seemed to pass between them.

"John Thomas says not everywhere. But can't he?" Two pairs of round blue eyes fastened on her, looking for the final word.

"He can go several places he couldn't without the ramp. But some things will still be hard, like going over rough ground, or getting into a buggy, or going up into the hay loft."

"So we must pray for him and help him any way we

can," Mammi added, always ready to teach her young ones what it meant to be a neighbor.

The twins nodded solemnly, and Miriam and her mother exchanged glances, sharing a little amusement mixed with a great deal of love.

As her mother's gaze lingered on Miriam's face, Miriam realized she hadn't hidden her worries entirely. No one else might have noticed, but Mammi always did.

"If I had a pulley and a rope, I could figure out a way to get Matt up to the loft." A spark of excitement lit Sammy's eyes, as if he pictured trying it out himself.

"No." Daad's voice was firm.

"But, Daadi…"

"No, Sammy. And don't go trying it on yourself, you hear?"

Sammy nodded, convinced and disappointed.

Miriam had to hide a smile. Mammi always said that Sammy had more dangerous ideas in one day than the rest of the kinder did in a year.

Eventually Daad and the boys scattered to their morning chores, and Miriam stacked dishes quickly. "I'll help with these. I have time before I leave."

A few minutes later, her hands plunged into the hot soapy water, the words spilled out.

"You know something's wrong, yah? Did you hear about the trial?"

Mammi rinsed a plate and started to dry it. "So that's it. I thought it might be. I heard something when I was in the grocery store yesterday. How is Matthew taking it?"

"He doesn't know yet." She scrubbed the oatmeal kettle so hard that soapsuds splattered her face, and she had to rub them away with her wrist. "At least, he didn't when I left. Abel had gotten a letter about it, and he dreaded telling him."

"He's worried about it, and no wonder." Mammi's forehead wrinkled. "Those poor things. To have to go through hearing all about it again just when they were starting to heal…it seems unfair."

"Yah, it does. It will hurt all of them, Matthew worst of all, maybe. I think he imagines sometimes that he could have avoided the accident. That's foolish, but no amount of telling can change his feelings. Physically he's been doing so well, but…"

Mammi patted her shoulder. "Ach, I know. You've worked hard to help him. You're afraid it will set him back, ain't so?"

"For sure." Her heart seemed to twist. "Yesterday he was so encouraged after he managed to stand on his own. He told me he'd do everything he could to get as well as possible. He just wants to be useful."

Mammi nodded, understanding. "It will be gut for him to feel he's able to help, even if he can't run the farm by himself. It would be for anyone. When we can help, we feel valuable."

Miriam reflected that her mother's understanding of people had shaped how she raised her children. Somehow she'd never seen that in her before, and she'd certain sure never appreciated it. Mammi had taught all of them that being useful was what God wanted of us, even if no one else ever appreciated it.

Miriam rinsed a dish and put it in the rack. "You didn't tell me what people were saying at the market."

"No." Mammi hesitated for a moment. "Most folks I talked to were feeling bad for the King family. But I heard someone had written to the newspaper saying that the Amish buggies were a danger on the road."

Temper flaring, Miriam slapped a bowl into the drainer so hard she feared she'd broken it. "I don't know why people think they have to say such things. If Matt heard that, he'd feel even more responsible, and it's not fair. After all, that boy had been drinking."

He'd been just sixteen, almost the same age as David. Boys balancing on the edge of being men, swaying first one way and then the other and sometimes falling. Like Wayne, the boy she'd worked with in Ohio. Her heart ached for all of them, including the young driver.

Mammi seemed to be reading her thoughts. "Drinking or not, I don't suppose he meant to do wrong. He was young and reckless, and his parents must have been worrying and praying about him, just as we do about your bruders."

"I know." Miriam wiped her eyes with the corner of a dishcloth. "I guess there's not so much difference between parents, whether they're Amish or Englisch. Now all of it will be in the newspapers, and everyone will talk about it."

Wiping the last plate, Mammi set it down carefully. "Has Matthew been able to forgive him?"

No need to ask who she meant. "I don't think so," she said unhappily. "I know the bishop has been coming to counsel him, but Matt…well, he's holding on to the pain, I'd say. When Tim asked me to try to find out what's holding him back, I didn't have much trouble seeing that his lack of forgiveness was part of it."

"Part?"

"Yah." Miriam dried her hands slowly, her thoughts busy. "He feels guilty, I know that. Guilty and useless."

"That's a hurtful combination. Hurtful to him, I mean."

"Yah." She held back for a moment, and then the words burst out. "What can I do? It's like…like watching an accident happening and not being able to stop it. The trial will come, the King family will go through their pain and grief all over again, and I'm afraid Matt will go backwards instead of forwards. Back to staring at the ceiling in bitterness."

Mammi turned to her, dropping the dish towel. "My sweet girl, you can't stop what's going to happen. All you can do is help them through it. Matthew depends on you—I could see that yesterday. Even if you're just there to stand beside him, it will help."

Would it? Miriam was frozen with doubt. Was she wise enough, strong enough, to make a difference?

Then her mother's arms went around her, hugging her tightly, and she knew she had to try.

The new day was cooler, making everyone more energetic, and Matt still hung on to the hopefulness he'd found the previous day. He didn't have any illusions about becoming the man he'd been before the accident, but if he could improve enough to be of some use around the farm, he'd try to be satisfied with that.

He wheeled himself out of his room, maneuvering the chair easily. He'd go out on the porch and try out the ramp again. Maybe surprise Miriam by being outside when she got there.

The house was so still that he thought no one was in the kitchen. Then he heard Mamm's and Daad's low voices. He was about to speak when he heard what Daad was saying.

"He has to be told, Elizabeth. Better he hears it from us rather than anyone else."

"No one would tell—" Mammi began.

"Would tell me what?" Matt propelled himself into the room with one powerful push of the wheels. "What has happened?"

Mammi looked at him, pressed her lips together, and turned away. Tears had welled in her eyes, alarming him.

"Daad?" He shoved his chair closer. "Was ist letz?"

"We've heard something about the accident. The driver is going on trial—you know that, yah?"

"I know. The police said they'd pass on what I told them about what happened."

He gritted his teeth together. He'd still been in the hospital then, hardly over the shock of the accident. Just beginning to understand how badly he was hurt.

"They say it may start as early as next week or the following one." Daad frowned at the paper he held in his hand and then thrust it toward Matt. "You'd best see what it says for yourself."

Matt stared at the letter, forcing his mind to absorb it all before he reacted. But he couldn't, because after the news about when and where it might happen, he saw something more.

"This says they want to talk to me. The district attorney's office will send someone to ask me some questions." He fluttered the paper. "Why? What do they think I can tell them that I didn't say before?"

Daad shook his head. "Maybe something wasn't clear. I thought… I hoped, anyway, that the driver would admit his guilt. That it would all be settled quickly instead of—"

He seemed to choke on the words, and Matt finished for him. "Instead of dragging it all out again. Making us relive it. Putting it in the newspaper so everyone is talking."

The emotions that spurted up seemed strong enough to power him out of the chair, even out of the room. Why? Why did they have to go through it?

"That is justice," Daad said heavily, answering the question Matt hadn't asked out loud. "Our faith tells us to cooperate with the law unless it runs against God's law."

He knew that just as well as his father did, but rebellion still roiled in him. He turned away, not wanting Daad to see the feelings in his face, and his eyes caught a bit of movement through the screen door. Miriam stood there, her hand raised to the handle, her eyes wide.

"You might as well come in. I suppose you've heard about this already."

Miriam stepped inside, her gaze going from Daad's solemn face to Mamm's tearful one and then to his, no doubt showing anger.

"I'm sorry. I've come at a bad time. Do you want me..." She gestured toward the door, a question in her voice.

"Stay, please." His father had contrived to sound calm. "Matthew shouldn't miss his therapy because of this." He held out his hand to take the letter, but Matt shook his head.

"This says I'm supposed to tell them when someone can come and talk to me about the accident."

His mother made a soft, pained sound and reached out as if groping for support. Before he or Daad could do anything, Miriam had gone to her, clasping her hand.

"It's all right, Elizabeth. You won't have to talk to them."

He wanted to flare up. To ask her what she knew about it. But whatever she knew or didn't know about the legal system, she'd known what to do about his mother.

"Yah, that's right, Mammi. Why don't you sit down? Is there any coffee left from breakfast?"

"I'll get it." Miriam helped her mother sit at the table, and in another moment had brought the coffee, pouring for Mamm and Daad. She held the pot out to him questioningly.

He shook his head, and she set it down.

"I'll get the equipment ready while you talk," she murmured.

"No, stay." He wasn't sure why he wanted her presence. Maybe because she could probably stop him before he upset Mamm any further. Or maybe for him, because she would understand.

"You'll have to talk to this person," Daad said. "It wouldn't be right to refuse."

Matt had to push down a tangle of emotions so he could speak calmly. "I can't tell them any more than I said before," he repeated. "I wish they'd leave us alone." He slapped his hand down on the table.

Daad shook his head. "We must do what's required." He passed his hand across his eyes as if to shut out the pictures the letter must have brought to mind.

Matt had a few of his own, pounding to get in. Seeing the buggy smashed on top of him. Hearing the horse whinny in pain. Trying to turn his head, to see David. And—

His hands clenched into fists. "I can't forgive, but I don't want revenge. I just want to be left alone."

Daad shook his head again. He was right, of course, but the rightness of it didn't change Matt's feelings.

"If you talk to this person, you might be able to find out what's going to happen," Miriam said.

He shot an angry look at her. She winced, but she went on.

"It would help all of you to be prepared for it, ain't so?" Miriam said softly, probably expecting a harsh reply.

Matt glared at her. He didn't want to be prepared. He wanted to shout the words at her.

But he had just enough control to think that maybe

she had a point. If they understood what was coming, it might help Mamm, if not him. Maybe they could even get her to go to her sister's place until all this was over. If she and Betsy could be kept away from the whole thing, it would be easier to stand.

Was that what Miriam had meant? She looked so calm that he felt an instinct to rattle her. He wanted to throw something across the room and smash it. Smash it the way his fragile hope had been smashed.

He remembered her reaction to the jar of flowers. It would take more than that to rattle Miriam. That gentle, peaceful exterior of hers hid a core of iron.

By the time they were nearing the end of Matt's afternoon exercises, it seemed to Miriam that the King family had begun to adjust to the trial looming ahead of them. She could hear voices and the clink of jars from the kitchen where Elizabeth and Betsy were making corn relish. Abel and Joshua had vanished toward the upper field after the noon meal, talking easily about the work to be done.

As for Matt, he was concentrating fiercely on his attempts to take a step or two holding on to the bars. Beyond that concentration, she had the sense that his emotions were bubbling up, still ready to explode.

"Let go," he demanded, his arms rigid, muscles straining. "I can take a step without you holding on to me like I'm a baby trying to walk."

"And if you fall and crack your head against the bar? It'll be my fault. I don't want everybody mad at me."

She understood his frustration, but his mind wasn't in the right place just now to take chances.

"Tell them I insisted. Tell them I knocked your arm away. Tell them anything, but let me try at least one step."

Maybe she'd best let him try. If she didn't, he'd probably be doing it the instant her back was turned, and nobody would be there to break his fall.

"If I do, I'll stay close enough to—"

He was already shaking his head. "Stand back. I'll take my chances."

"I won't," she said flatly. "Either I'm in a position to grab you, or else I'll take the bars away entirely."

Matt glared at her, and she glared back. After a moment, his expression began to falter. His lips twitched. "Never met such a stubborn woman," he muttered. "All right. If you get hurt, don't blame me."

"I'm supposed to say that." She moved closer, her hand pressing on the long, flat muscles of his back. She took a shaky breath and braced herself. "Say when you're ready, and I'll let go."

His chest moved as he inhaled a deep breath. She focused on his arms. As long as they didn't fail him, he'd manage. Even if he faltered, he should be able to catch himself.

"Now," he said, waiting until he felt her hands move away. He looked down at his weakest leg, frowning in grim concentration. Muscles tightening, he forced his foot forward. Straining, he brought the other up to meet it.

Delighted, she grasped him again. None too soon, as his left arm began to buckle.

"There, now. Enough." She pulled the wheelchair up behind him, using her foot. "That's great."

He let her lower him back to the chair. "I did it." He said the words evenly, with no hint of yesterday's triumph and exhilaration. She felt a different determination in him now, and his face settled into fierce lines.

Miriam pulled the chair away from the bars. "Now relax. Do you want some juice?" She nodded toward the bottle on the bedside table.

"Yah, guess I could use some." He leaned back, and when she put the glass into his hand, his fingers trembled a little. Small wonder. It was all she could do to keep hers steady.

He drank deeply, and then looked at her, his eyes studying her face. "You're worried. Why?"

She could only be honest with him. He'd recognize any attempt to steer him away.

"I'm afraid this hassle about the trial will hold back your progress. It's a pretty big distraction, ain't so?"

His face clouded. "Makes all of us remember too much. No, that's not it. I certain sure haven't forgotten anything that happened that day, but it was like a…like a mist, I guess, shielding it. Now—"

Matt fell silent, his lips clamping on the word.

His pain seemed to ricochet through her, clamping around her heart. "I know," she said softly. "Even when the memories are good ones, it makes your throat get tight and your eyes sting."

"And these are all bad. No, no that's not right.

Even that day, even minutes before the car hit, we were laughing." His voice roughened, but he went on. "David was teasing me about not getting married yet. Saying he'd better hurry up and start courting someone so Mammi wouldn't worry about not having grandchildren."

"I can almost hear him. He always had laughter lurking in his eyes, ain't so? That's why everyone loved him."

Now her voice was choking up. Matt reached out, clutching her hand so tightly it hurt.

"He was so young. He had everything to look forward to. It's not fair."

"I know, I know," she murmured. Her thoughts raced to other young boys who stood balanced between childhood and manhood. "Boys that age are on the edge of turning into men, and sometimes they're so daring or so careless you wonder how they'll make it."

"David wasn't daring," he said quickly.

"No, but the driver was. He wasn't much older than David."

She winced as his grasp became even tighter.

"Are you saying I should forgive him?" Anger broke into his voice.

"Ach, Matt, that is between you and God. But I can't help thinking that he was just a boy, too. And now his life is wrecked, and his parents are grieving." She shook her head, trying to hold back tears. "It seems too big for anyone to heal it but God."

Matt seemed to mull over her words. Then he shook his head. His grip loosened, and he looked down at her hand with a muffled exclamation. "I'm sorry." He smoothed gentle fingers over the angry red marks.

"It's all right." She tried to draw her hand away, but stopped when she saw that now he seemed to draw some comfort from her touch.

Matt let out a long breath. "Daad says we must forgive." His eyes darkened, not in anger but in pain. "I can try to understand what they're feeling, but I don't know that I can ever forgive."

Chapter Eleven

Matt had been up early on Saturday morning, watching from the window as Daad and Joshua left for the co-op. Sales would be brisk today, and they didn't want to miss the buyers. Restaurant owners wanted the freshest of the produce for their weekend customers, and they'd be there in force.

The house seemed unusually quiet after the breakfast dishes were done, and he found he was waiting for the sounds of Miriam's arrival. Funny, to be so eager for something to happen. For a long time after the accident, he hadn't noticed or cared. Now he was restless, eager to be doing, if only he could find something useful.

He was about to head out to the porch when he heard a sound from the living room. For a moment his brain couldn't identify it, but even as he turned, he knew. Someone was crying. The sound was muffled, but unmistakable.

His heart lurched. If it was his mother, he was helpless. Comforting Mammi would be such a reversal of their roles that he couldn't imagine coping with it. Still, he had to do something. Steeling himself, he pushed the chair toward the room.

The wheelchair made little sound as it rolled forward. The person who sat on the floor in front of the cupboard clearly didn't hear him. It was Betsy, bending forward over clasped hands, her bowed back shaking with the force of her sobs.

Matt moved closer, wheels bumping against the boxes of games and puzzles she'd obviously pulled out of the cabinet. He reached out to clasp her shoulder.

"Was ist letz? Are you hurt, Betsy?" What could there be about puzzles and games to make her weep?

She jumped in reaction and shook her head, not looking at him.

"Something is making you cry. Komm, tell me about it. Troubles are easier to bear when they're shared, ain't so?" His own words startled him. They sounded like something Miriam would say. Or Mammi, before the world had shattered.

A stubborn shake of the head was Betsy's only answer. She mopped at her face with the backs of her hands, and then seemed to realize that she had to say something.

"It's nothing. I'm okay."

She obviously wasn't, and he'd run out of things to say. He longed for someone else to walk in and handle this…someone like Miriam or Mammi. He even looked toward the door. Nothing.

"Where's Mammi?" She'd know what to do.

"She…she went across the road to take some to-matoes to Great-Aunt Alice. And some shoofly pie."

That explained her absence. Mammi's aunt and uncle occupied a small house back a long lane across the road, and normally she made regular treks to check on them, usually carrying food. It was encouraging that she'd begun to do it again, but he could wish she'd waited a day or two.

Betsy stacked several games. "I'm supposed to clean up the cabinet while she's gone. I'd best get it done." She grabbed the stack and turned to shove them back on the shelf. As she did, something fell from her lap and landed in front of him.

His stomach lurched. Not just something. It was a carved wooden fish—the brook trout he'd carved for David's birthday last year. He remembered the feel of it in his hands even without touching it…the way he'd used the smallest of his chisels to add the tiny ridges that were the scales. He bent to pick it up.

A year ago David had still been with them. He'd loved to fish…loved walking up the creek in the early morning to the pool where he always found some "brookies."

His fingers moved on the curve of the fish's back, remembering David's expression when he'd unwrapped it. "Where…" He cleared his throat. "Where did you find this?"

"It was behind the boxes. I don't know how it got there." Tears threatened to fall again. She screwed up her face in an attempt to hold them back. "Remember?

You said you were going to make your gifts from now on, and David said he'd have to remind you."

"Yah." His voice was husky. Betsy remembered even better than he did. He held the fish a moment longer, and then he leaned forward and dropped it in her lap.

"You should keep it. He'd want you to have it. Komm, let's get this stuff put away before Mammi gets back." He handed her a game at random, trying not to look at the fish. He'd longed to keep it himself, but he thought maybe his little sister needed it more.

A glimpse of movement through the front window alerted him. "Here comes Mammi. I'll finish these. You run upstairs and put some cold water on your eyes. No sense worrying Mammi."

Betsy scrambled to her feet, holding the fish against her. Impulsively she leaned forward to press her cheek against his, and then she was gone, running up the stairs.

It was simple enough to shove the remaining games in and shut the door on them. He was back in the kitchen by the time Mammi came in.

"Your aunt and onkel send their love," she said, putting her basket down. "Do you want anything before Miriam comes to start your exercises?"

He shook his head. "I think I'll wait for her out on the porch."

But when he reached the porch, he headed straight for the ramp and started down. Miriam would be here soon, but there was something he wanted to do first.

He reached the bottom of the ramp safely and headed toward the shed next to the lower level of the barn.

The lane wasn't so bad—there was enough gravel on it to give some stability to the chair. Lots more arm muscle required to move, but doable.

Then he turned to the grassy slope that led to the shed, got about three feet and stuck. Muttering to himself, he bent to check the wheels, only to find the right front one had hit a soft patch and sunk in. Just a little, but enough to stop him.

He leaned the other way, pushing the wheels, feeling the strain on his arm muscles. The chair tilted…he thought for an instant he was going over. Then someone grabbed it, pulling it as he leaned back.

The chair settled, and Miriam let out a long whoosh of air. "What are you doing?"

In an instant, Miriam regretted the sharpness of her tone. She leaned against the chair, trying to calm the shakiness that set in once she knew Matt was all right.

"Just give me a hand." He pointed. "There. The shed. Get me over there." He slapped the side of the chair in frustration.

Miriam pressed her lips together. "Wheelchairs aren't great on rough ground. Whatever you want, can't I get it for you?"

He didn't answer—just planted his hands on the wheels, gripping them so hard she could see the cords of muscle on his forearms. "Are you going to help me or not?"

Maybe counting to ten would help. Or maybe not. "Okay. We'll both have to push."

It actually wasn't as bad as she'd feared. Apparently the wet spot he'd hit was the only one, and the wheels bounced over the clumps of grass to the shed.

"There." She started to reach for the door latch, but he was ahead of her. He leaned out of the chair to yank it open.

The only light in the interior was what came from the door and slipped through the cracks between the boards. As Miriam's eyes grew accustomed to the dim light, she realized it was a wood storage, stacked along the back wall with split firewood.

"I hope we're not going to build a fire," she said. "I think it'll be hot enough without it."

Matt's concentration finally wavered, and he looked at her as if he saw her now. "Yah, I don't think we'll need one." His expression eased, but he still seemed intent on something. "Look over on the left wall. See that old fruit box?"

"You want something from it?" she asked as she stepped inside, holding her skirt away from the cobweb that draped the opening.

"Just pull the whole thing over here so I can see it. Or do you need some help?" His tone was teasing, as if with his target in sight, he didn't need to snap out orders.

She'd grasped the end of the box by then, and she looked back at him. "I don't think I'm that weak."

She gave it a yank and dragged the box out into the light. This time she'd managed to hit the spider web, and she had to brush it from her skirt and then wipe the remnants from her hand onto the grass.

The box was half-full of what seemed a miscellaneous collection of wood…most of the pieces fairly small, some of them twisted roots, some knotty bits of misshapen limbs. She stood and looked at it as Matt bent to scrabble through them.

He looked up at her and lifted his eyebrows. "You don't understand yet? But you were the one who mentioned wood-carving, ain't so?"

The light dawned. "Yah, for sure. But are these the pieces you picked out to carve?"

Matt chuckled at the doubt in her voice. "You don't just start with a block of wood. At least, I don't." He picked up one piece, turning it over in his hands and running his fingers along its curves. "My grossdaadi taught me. He always said that the figure was already there in the wood. You just had to see it. Then you take away all the parts that don't belong."

She loved the way his face warmed when he talked about his grandfather. They must have been close in the way that sometimes happened between generations. Her own grandmother was close to her that way.

He picked up another piece and put it in her hands. "Go on, take a good look at it. Turn it around and see what you can feel with your fingertips."

Miriam tried, but it might have been easier if his hand weren't guiding hers, warm against her skin.

"Feel that bump there, and the other one on this side." He guided her fingers. "Think about what might have that shape in it. Or this part that sticks out, and then curves under."

It seemed to take shape in her mind as he talked. The rounded part, almost like a jaw. "I see. It's like a head, or maybe a face."

"Gut. What kind of head? What could the bumps be?"

"Horns? Ears?" She laughed. "I don't think I'm very good at this."

"You're doing fine." He squeezed her hand and released it, taking the wood piece. "This might be a deer's head, or even a rabbit with the ears standing up. Once you decide, then it's not hard."

"It would be for me, I'm afraid. What made you decide to start on this?"

His face sobered, the laughter fading from it. "Betsy." He hesitated a moment. "She found a fish that I had carved for David's last birthday. It brought up a lot of memories."

"For both of you, I guess." She studied his face, wondering how much she should question.

"Yah. Funny," he said, but his expression said it wasn't humorous. "I was thinking that I'd like to keep it, and then I saw her face. She needed it more than I did."

"That was thoughtful." She couldn't keep herself from resting her hand on his arm. "She's struggling, I think."

"Yah. Anyway, I remembered I'd intended to make something for her next birthday, but by then…"

She understood. By then they were all grieving, groping their way through pain.

"Betsy would love to have it anytime. It doesn't have to be a birthday gift. What will you make?"

Matt fingered the piece of wood that he'd picked out. "You know what I see in here? Not a deer or a rabbit, but an owl." He turned it the other way, so that he could trace a flat round area with a few smooth, smaller rounds inside it. "There's the face, and here are the eyes. Don't you see?"

To her surprise, she did see the face of an owl emerging from the wood. She glanced at his intent face.

"It means something special?" she ventured. "The owl?"

He leaned back in the chair, seeming to look back in time. "Betsy might not remember. But I think she will. David and I took her walking up in the woods when she was maybe five or six. We came upon a barn owl sitting on a limb just over our heads." He smiled, picturing it. "She was so excited because it was just like an owl in a story Mammi had been reading to her, with its white face like a heart."

She nodded, understanding. The same book was probably on her family's shelves, too.

"Usually they fly away at the sight or sound of people, but this one just sat there for another minute while she talked about it. Then it swooped away." He shook his head, smiling. "She must have talked about it for a week, and Mammi had to read the book to her over and over."

"You remember. I'd say she'd remember, too."

He released the brake on the chair. "Just shove that box back inside the door and let's go in. I want to start on it."

She did as he asked, then flipped the latch on the door.

"We'll go inside, but carving will have to wait until after your exercises."

"Carving first," he said, his eyes laughing at her.

"Exercises first," she said firmly, giving the chair a push.

"Bossy," he muttered, but he was smiling.

His smile was infectious, but Miriam had even more making her happy. Despite the looming pressure of the trial, Matt had seen someone else's pain. More than that, he'd done something about it.

She murmured a soundless prayer that this might be a good step towards healing, both for him and for his little sister.

Matt couldn't figure out why he was in such a good mood right now, not when the trial was hanging over them. A month ago he'd have said he couldn't feel that way unless he was back to normal, and now he was celebrating the smallest step forward.

He studied Miriam's face as she got everything ready for his workout. He couldn't deny that Miriam had something to do with the change in him. Her faith in his progress must have been contagious, that's all. He certain sure couldn't have drummed it up by himself.

The question of the lawyer, the looming shadow of

the trial…well, they were still there. But for the moment, he could shove them into the back of his mind and concentrate on what was in front of him.

The worries of the day are enough for the day. That was what his grandfather used to say. He'd been right.

"Ready?" Miriam indicated the rack of hand weights. "Let's get started."

As they worked their way through the exercises, Matt considered how much his opinion of Miriam had changed over what was really a short time, compared with the fact that he'd known her all their lives.

"I always thought you were so quiet. What changed?"

Laughter lit her eyes. "Maybe you just weren't noticing before. Or my brothers were making too much noise. Sometimes it wonders me how Mammi can know each of us so well when there are so many of us, but she does."

He considered that. "I'd have said the same about Mammi, but…" He struggled with what he wanted to convey. "It seemed like she got lost when David died."

Miriam paused, putting down the exercise band she was holding. "I guess that's right. She was confronted with something so bad that she didn't know where she was for a while."

"I didn't make it any easier. I must be about the worst person you've ever worked with, yah?"

Smiling, she shook her head. "Not even close. You never met the boy I worked with out in Ohio." She sobered, her clear eyes shadowed suddenly. "He shook my confidence more than anything else." She shrugged. "But there's no use dwelling on spilled milk."

Matt grasped her hand before she could turn away. "Something happened…something that upsets you when you think about it. If you want to talk…"

She looked down at his hand, but she didn't pull away. "I don't think it's a good idea."

"Why not? I've unloaded on you plenty."

"That's different," she said quickly. "You're the patient, and anything that troubles you can affect your progress."

"And you're my friend, since we were about three or four. Isn't that just as important as being a patient?"

Her face lightened as she seemed to hear the affection that was behind the words. "Yah, well, I guess. Maybe I'd just gotten too confident. The boy was hard to work with at first. He was only fifteen, and he was cut off from everything his friends were doing. He had an illness that affected his joints and muscles. Sometimes he'd be better, his mother told me, but then he'd get worse again. But I felt like I was making good progress with him."

"Something happened?" he asked gently, knowing by her expression she was getting onto shaky territory.

"I guess I'd been thinking about him like he was one of my little brothers. Then I found out that he… well, he had a crush on me. And he thought I felt the same about him."

"Poor kid." He spoke automatically, and then realized the meaning of what he'd said. To be thinking that Miriam—sweet, strong Miriam—loved you and then learning you were wrong would be devastating.

He wanted to say something of that to her, but he

couldn't. He couldn't because he was beginning to see something he hadn't even guessed at, and he had to know for sure before he spoke.

While he sat there, silent, she must have decided that he wasn't interested, because she shrugged, and her voice changed. "Well, it's not such a big thing, I guess, but it certain sure damaged my confidence. I thought I'd found my gift, you see, and I'd stumbled badly. His parents were so angry—"

"But even if you made a mistake, well, that doesn't mean it isn't your talent. You're still learning, ain't so?"

"I hope." Her fingers tightened on his hand for a moment. "I want to do the thing God put me here for."

"Yah." It struck him that she was saying what he'd been feeling. "But what happens if you really can't do that thing any longer?" The bitterness sprang out of hiding and nipped at him. That was where he was.

"I don't know, Matthew." She didn't pretend not to understand him. "Maybe you have to find a different way of using your gift. Or maybe you have another gift that's equally important."

"Maybe." But he doubted it.

As if she thought it was time to distract him, she put away the equipment they'd been using. "Why don't we take a break and get your carving set up?"

Without waiting for an answer, she pulled out the table they'd pushed against the wall, and set out the wooden piece they'd brought in and the roll of tools. "What else do you need?"

He didn't intend to be switched away from the con-versation, but in spite of himself, the sight of his materials stirred a need he hadn't even recognized he was feeling.

"This is enough to start with," he muttered, unwrapping his tools and smoothing them with the soft fabric of the case. He drew out his favorite knife, and it felt comfortable and familiar in his hand.

He glanced up at Miriam and smiled, liking the way her face lit in response.

"Good?" she asked.

"Yah. This one's what I use most often."

She leaned closer and reached out to touch the blade.

"Careful, it's sharp."

She drew her finger away after touching it gingerly. "I'll say. I hope you're careful with it."

"You get used to working with it." He smiled. "The first time Grossdaadi let me use it, I cut myself in the first five minutes. Mammi was mad, but Grossdaadi just said, 'This time he'll be more careful,' and I was. You can't work with it if it's not sharp. See?" He made the first slice, and a sliver of wood curled away. "Like butter."

Once started, it came back to him. His hands remembered the use of the tools, and a satisfaction he hadn't felt in months seeped through him.

Miriam moved, murmuring something about helping his mother, but he shook his head and pointed with the knife. "Sit and relax. You don't have to be always working."

She subsided onto the chair, seeming perfectly content to sit still and watch. In fact, there was a quality of stillness about it that was soothing.

They sat without talking as he worked and she watched. The figure had just begun to emerge from the wood. And then the door burst open and Betsy propelled herself into the room, her face excited.

"You won't believe it, Matt. There was a message on the machine from the courthouse. It was some lawyer, and he said he'd be here to talk to you on Monday morning." She sounded impressed. "What do you think of that?"

He didn't speak for a moment. Nothing he said could match Betsy's excitement. He found he was looking automatically at Miriam for her reaction.

She looked the way he felt—as if something that had been looming over them was here.

Chapter Twelve

Miriam sat on the backless bench in the Gauses' barn on Sunday, trying to concentrate on the voice of the bishop. Unfortunately she wasn't having much success. The heat of the late August day didn't trouble her, despite the red faces of those around her. At least a slight breeze came through the double doors that had been slid open. No, it was her restless heart that caused the problem.

Next to her, cousin Lyddy fidgeted a bit, controlled herself and then looked across to the opposite side of the barn where Simon Fisher sat with his little daughter. Miriam understood. Lyddy was longing to be with Simon and his daughter, soon to be hers, too.

Happy as she was for Lyddy, that didn't keep her mind away from Matt. They had been having such a blessed, peaceful time together the previous day, with Matthew carving while she sat and watched the deft, sure movements of his hands.

But then news of the lawyer's visit had exploded all

their peace. Not that Matt had reacted openly, but she could sense his feelings without the need for words. Matt was torn between a resurgence of his anger, the pain of his grief and probably the endless struggle to forgive.

She heard again his voice saying he didn't think he could forgive. But if that was true, how could he move on with his life? And how much would that inward struggle affect his physical recovery?

She could no longer tell herself she was interested only as his aide, because she knew it wasn't true. She loved him—loved him in a way she'd never imagined it would be possible to love someone. Every day it continued to grow.

Maybe nothing would ever come of that love. She'd had no indication that he felt anything but friendship for her. But if she could help him become whole again, that was enough reward for her.

She slid to her knees for the final prayer and blessing. Then, as people began to move, Lyddy smiled and spoke. "I'm wilted, I think. But look at Grossmammi. She's as fresh as a daisy. How does she do it?"

Miriam glanced behind her and saw what Lyddy meant. Grossmammi was already talking with her cronies, while around them the men began carrying tables and benches out under the trees. Not a strand of her snowy-white hair was out of place, and her skin glowed with the joy she felt at being here.

"Maybe that's the fruit of a good life," Miriam suggested, and Lyddy laughed.

"Then we might be in trouble. Seriously, how is

Matt doing? I see Abel and Elizabeth are both here this morning."

"He's improving," she said, with a silent prayer that it might continue. "Yah, they left Betsy in charge this morning."

"Was that a gut idea? She can be so flighty at times."

Not any longer, Miriam thought. The accident had pushed her to grow up in a hurry. Maybe too much so.

"I'm sure she's glad to be relied upon," Miriam said. "She really loves helping Matt. I just hope Elizabeth isn't fretting to be home."

"It's gut for her to be out after all this time," Lyddy said, and they both watched as friends surrounded Elizabeth, all eager to greet her.

"Time to get busy," Lyddy said as they stepped out into the open. "I said I'd help carry things to the table."

"I'll come, too," Miriam said, pausing a moment to enjoy the fresh breeze that cooled her face. It rustled the corn stalks in the nearest field so that it sounded as if they talked to each other. She amused herself for a moment, thinking what they might say, and then headed for the farmhouse in Lyddy's wake.

She had almost caught up when Nola Frey hurried to her. Miriam stiffened, ready for anything. Nola, like Hilda Berger and one or two others here, had relatives in the community Miriam had visited. She'd probably have heard any rumors that were going around by now.

But Nola was smiling, at least. "Ach, it's gut to see you this morning, Miriam. My cousin wanted me to say she was sorry not to have a chance to visit you again before you left. She said you went all of a sudden."

There was a questioning note in the comment that Miriam didn't miss. She planted a smile on her face. "I'd actually planned to leave weeks earlier, but I stayed on because another family needed some help. But I was wonderful eager to get home by then. It felt like years."

"I see." Her eyes were still curious. "But surely…"

"Goodness, I promised to help bring the food out. I must get busy. My best to your family." She hurried off before she could be stopped.

As she scurried away, she let out a long breath. Nola had been fishing, no doubt about it, but at least Miriam hadn't lost her poise. Maybe Nola would have forgotten about it by the next time Miriam talked to her, or some new exciting story would replace it.

She crossed paths with Lyddy, who carried large baskets filled with sandwiches. "Better hurry, or everything will be done," she teased.

"Right, I will." Even as she neared the door, she passed several younger girls carrying more sandwich fillings and two more with large dishes of gelatin salads. Lifting a hand in greeting, she slipped up the steps to the porch and reached for the screen door. And then she froze at the sound of her name from within.

"…says that Miriam is devoted to helping Matthew get well. She said you wouldn't believe how much help she is with him."

"The end of it will be that he'll marry her," another voice declared.

Someone else exclaimed at that. "Surely not. I thought it was Liva Ann…"

"That's all over, I hear. She couldn't stand marrying someone all scarred up like that, with her being so pretty and all. But Miriam wouldn't mind. After all, she doesn't have so many choices, not at her age. If she's ever going to get married, this is her chance, and she won't hesitate to grab it. You'll see…"

Miriam couldn't listen anymore. Shaking, she moved silently the porch and stopped at the nearest table, hanging on to it for a moment to steady her ragged breathing.

So that was what people were saying. That Matthew was her last chance, and she'd be foolish not to grab him.

She drew in a steadying breath. If that were so, she wouldn't marry at all. Better to live alone the rest of her life than to be married only for her nursing ability to a man she loved with all her heart.

The tension in the air Monday while they waited for the attorney to show up, Matt decided, was like waiting to be released from the hospital. The whole family sat around the table, seeming unable to start anything else until this was over. Even Daad had allowed Josh to begin the day's work without him and sat drinking a third or fourth cup of coffee.

At a step on the porch, Daad's hand jerked, and the coffee sloshed over.

"It's Miriam," Matt said quickly, recognizing her step. He'd known she'd get here before the attorney would.

She came in, hesitating as the door closed and she

realized everyone was looking at her. "Is something wrong?"

He shook his head. "No, but you can help me settle something. I don't think the rest of the family should be in on my discussion with the attorney, especially Mammi and Betsy."

"We are your family and David's," Mammi said quickly. "I, at least, should hear what he says. Betsy is too young—"

"No, I'm not!" Betsy was offended, that was certain sure.

Miriam seemed to understand instantly what he wanted. She moved quietly to his mother and touched her shoulder, smiling at Betsy to include her.

"It will be difficult for Matthew to talk about the accident to the man, ain't so? And even more painful if he knows you are hearing it, too. He will have trouble talking in front of you. You understand, ain't so?"

Miriam had said exactly the right thing, as he'd known she would. Mammi hesitated, looking from Miriam to him, and then at Daad.

"Miriam is right," Daadi said. "We don't want to make it harder on Matthew than it must be."

Mammi hesitated, undecided, and then the sound of a car pulling up grabbed everyone's attention. They listened, hardly breathing, Matt thought, as he approached.

In another few moments, the man from the district attorney's office was at the door, opening it in response to Daad's invitation to enter.

His youth was the first thing that struck Matt. For

sure too young to be a qualified attorney and working on something like this.

As if in response to Matt's thought, the young man stammered, trying to introduce himself. "I... I'm Robert Forman, from the district attorney's office. I'm here to see Matthew King."

He was slight and fair, looking as if he hadn't grown into his fine suit yet, and he had the sort of fair skin that blushed easily, making it a fiery red as he realized he was the target of so many eyes.

"I'm Matthew King." he said. It was up to him to deal with this, he knew. "These are my parents, Abel and Elizabeth King." A pause ensued while young Forman shook hands with Daad and nodded with the effect of a bow to Mamm.

"And here is my sister, Betsy, and Miriam Stoltzfus, who is..." He paused, unsure how to refer to her. Helper, friend, something more? "...my aide," he finished.

"I won't keep you any longer than I have to," Forman hurried on with what sounded like a prepared opening. "I appreciate your letting me come and see you." His gaze lingered on the wheelchair.

Matt shifted his weight, uncomfortable with his stare.

Maybe aware of his reaction, Forman flushed again. "If we can go over the facts of the accident and the statement you made, that will help us with our case. Is there somewhere...?" He looked around, clearly searching for privacy.

Daad rose. "We all have things to do, so we will

leave you here." He nodded to Mammi and Betsy, and after a moment's hesitation, they got up.

Miriam stirred, started to rise, and Matt stopped her with a hand on her arm. "I prefer that my aide stays with me."

"Um, yes, fine. I'm sure it's good if your aide is here, in case you need her." Forman flushed again and then sat in the chair Daad pulled out for him, setting his briefcase on the table and opening it.

The outside door closed behind the rest of the family, and they could hear the murmur of voices as they walked away.

Forman seemed to pull himself together, and Matt wondered how many times he'd done this sort of thing.

"Now, if you would just tell me about the accident the way you remember it, I'll follow along in the statement you signed when you were in the hospital. That way if you've remembered anything additional, I can make those changes."

Matt nodded to show he understood, but his nerves tightened. This wouldn't be easy, going through it all again. At least it would help that he'd talked through some of it with Miriam.

It struck him that he hadn't asked Miriam if she was willing to be here. He looked at her. "If you don't want…" he began.

She shook her head. "It's fine. I'd rather be here." Her eyes were apprehensive, but she patted his arm reassuringly. Maybe he was being selfish, but he accepted her help. He'd known he could count on her.

Forman spread his papers out on the table and

clicked his pen. "Now, if you'll just tell me about what you remember in your own words, that will be fine."

He cleared his throat and plunged in, like jumping into an icy pond.

"I was driving the buggy, and my brother, David, was sitting next to me. The road is hilly and curvy, but we were going slow, you understand?"

Forman nodded. "I took a ride over there to see the site."

"Good. We were talking, and I heard a car coming up behind me. It sounded as if it were coming pretty fast. So I steered the horse closer to the edge of the road…"

That much was easy. But as he talked his way through what had happened, the events became more and more vivid in his mind. Forman didn't speak, sometimes making a mark on the typescript in front of him.

Matt kept his voice was steady while he talked about the car striking the buggy, even of finding himself tangled in the wreckage, but he gripped Miriam's hand as if his life depended on holding on.

When he reached the moment that he'd glimpsed David's twisted body, though, his voice finally broke. He stopped, struggling for control.

After a moment, he glanced at the attorney and was surprised to see an expression of satisfaction on his face. What was there in this terrible telling to make anyone satisfied? He was suddenly repelled.

Miriam spoke, maybe to give him time. "You can

see that this is difficult, Mr. Forman. Since you have his statement already, is it really necessary?"

"Knowing the injured person makes a much stronger case against the defendant, don't you see?" he said eagerly. "If the jury hears the story from someone who suffered, they'll feel his pain."

Matt's revulsion deepened. "I don't want to make anyone else feel this way."

"Well, of course not," Forman said quickly, as if sensing he'd made a wrong step. "But you see, hearing directly from you makes it more likely that the defendant will get a harsher sentence. You'd be surprised at how lax juries can be."

"No doubt." He'd mastered his voice again, but not his feelings. They tumbled around in him confusingly, but one thing was suddenly very clear. "But they will not hear it from me. You have my statement of what happened. I don't want to testify."

That seemed to catch the attorney off guard. For an instant, Forman gaped, speechless. "But…but we thought for sure you'd want to speak. I know that sometimes Amish won't do it, but with the loss of your brother and your suffering—surely you want to see the defendant get a good stiff jail sentence for what he did."

"No." He knew his answer was final.

Matt found he was thinking about something Miriam said. Something about boys that age, boys like David, like the driver, even like her brothers, balancing on the line between being carefree, careless boys and being men.

He was vaguely aware of Forman talking, trying to

convince him, but it didn't matter. An accident could have been caused by any boy that age doing something stupid…any of them. His brother, hers… He couldn't do anything to help take the rest of that boy's life away from him.

The attorney ran out of arguments. "You're sure of that?" he asked.

"I'm sure. The law has my statement and will have to do with that. The driver will be held accountable according to the law, and we'll all get on with our lives."

Forman nodded, accepting his decision. "I understand, I guess." He sounded like a real person now, instead of one reciting a familiar speech.

"You do, don't you?" Miriam's voice startled him, she'd been so quiet. "If Matthew had to testify, if his family had to listen to it…well, that would be punishing them all over again."

Forman was intent upon her words. "When you put it like that, how could I help but understand?" His face relaxed, making him look no more than sixteen or seventeen himself.

"Good." Miriam smiled gently at him, as if he were a child who'd gotten something right.

He cleared his throat. "Well, I'd better tell you what might happen next. Since we won't have your testimony, the district attorney will probably agree on a plea bargain with the boy's lawyer. That means he'll admit he was at fault, and there will be a judge to decide the appropriate penalty." He looked a little anxious. "Do you understand?"

"I understand." Matt exchanged glances with Miriam. She looked relieved, and he realized that was what he felt, too. The heavy cloud that had loomed over them was gone.

"You shouldn't be troubled anymore, then. Although you might be asked if you want to make any statement to the judge."

He nodded, ready for the man to be gone.

In another moment, he had his wish. Miriam showed Forman to the door, standing there until the car turned and moved off down the driveway. Then she came back to him, smiling.

"You made up your mind, ain't so?"

"Yah." He struggled for a moment, knowing there was more he wanted to say, but not sure what or how. "I guess it is possible to forgive."

Chapter Thirteen

Miriam could only be thankful that this, at least, was over. Matt had not only stood up to the ordeal, but he had reached a decision, and with it, she hoped, the beginning of some peace.

She turned back to him from the screen door. "He's gone, and I see your mamm and daad coming." Another look told her that Matt was exhausted, and no wonder. She felt as if she'd been pressed through the wringer, and she didn't have Matt's painful memories.

Hurrying over, she put one hand on the table as she bent over him. "You…you must be tired out. Some coffee?"

He leaned back then, seeming to force his eyes to stay open. "Don't bother. I'm all right." He caught her hand as if to stop her, and she couldn't help but wince.

Startled, Matt moved it gently in his as he saw the red marks of his fingers. "I did that? I didn't know…"

"It's all right," she said quickly. "The marks will be gone by tomorrow." She tried to draw it away, but he held it in his, his finger tracing the marks with a featherlight touch.

"Matt…" she began, but couldn't find anything to say. Her throat was so tight she wouldn't have gotten words out anyway.

Matt's face twisted suddenly, as if he were hurt. Then he lifted her hand to his lips and kissed it, so quickly that it was over before she could react.

Footsteps sounded on the porch, and then his parents came in, looking at him with anxious eyes. Miriam drew her hand away and hid it in the folds of his skirt. No one else must see or exclaim.

Matt turned to his parents, somehow managing to smile. "It's all right. It's over. Where is Betsy?"

"Sulking," Abel said briefly. "She's hurt because you didn't let her stay with you, but it was no place for her."

It didn't take much for Miriam to fill in the rest of what had happened with Betsy. She'd been angry not only because she was excluded but also because Miriam had been allowed to stay. Maybe she would be blaming Miriam for it. Well, that was probably better than blaming her parents.

Abel moved to put his hand on his son's shoulder. "Are you all right?"

"Yah." Matt seemed to steel himself for what he had to say. "The man wanted me to go over what I'd said before. And then he wanted me to testify at the trial." His lips twisted. "He said that would make the jury punish the driver more. I told him I wouldn't. That's all."

"But…" Abel must have wanted more details, but he

seemed to recognize that now wasn't the time. "That's gut. You have done what the law required. But it is not for us to judge others."

Elizabeth wiped tears from her face and nodded. "The Lord says we must forgive, as He has forgiven us." Her expression quivered, and she turned away. "I must find Betsy." She went out, moving quickly.

Abel looked from his wife to his son, as if not knowing who to go to.

Matt made the decision for him. "Komm, Miriam. Let's get on with the exercises."

Relieved, Miriam hurried to open the door for him. Maybe she was being a coward, but Matt was the one she'd been hired to help. He had to come first.

When she began to organize the equipment, she actually had to stop and think about what to do first. It was as if her thoughts had been whipped up with a giant eggbeater.

Matt seemed equally distracted. He looked at her, then away. "Don't...don't do anything that will make you hand hurt. I can pick up the weights myself."

What was he thinking about? Was he remembering the moment when he'd pressed his lips to her palm? Was he regretting that he'd done it?

Maybe she ought to say something light about it, but how could she? So she contented herself with beginning the familiar routine.

Matt seemed to move through the exercises automatically, his mind elsewhere. At last they'd reached the bars. He was holding on to them, trying to force his leg to move forward, when suddenly he stopped.

She grabbed hold of him, bracing herself to bear his weight. If he fell—

He shook his head. "I have it. Bring the chair."

Pausing only to be sure he could support himself, Miriam pushed the wheelchair into place behind him. He sank into it, gripping the arms.

Possible explanations flew into her mind. "What is it? Do you feel dizzy? Sick?"

"I remembered."

She blinked, not following him. "Remembered what?"

He shoved the wheelchair around and gestured to the straight chair against the wall. "Sit down. I need to talk."

Matt was so intent that she didn't hesitate to do what he said. When she brought the chair, he moved so that they sat facing each other, knee to knee. His expression alarmed her, and she leaned toward him.

"You're sure you—"

Cutting her off with an impatient gesture, he began to speak. "Listen. When I was going over it all with the lawyer… I kept feeling like there was something more I should say. Something I should remember."

"Are you sure you don't want your daad to hear this?" She put her hand on his arm, and felt it as rigid as a steel bar.

He ignored the question except for a quick shake of the head. "There…when I stood up…it slid into my mind. The rest of the memory…what happened after I saw that I was trapped."

He didn't even seem aware of her now, but she didn't

dare move. "I heard it," he said. "I heard someone cry-ing."

Her voice was stuck in her throat. "David?" she whispered.

"No, not David. It was him…the driver."

"But he wasn't hurt…"

"He was crying and crawling into the wreckage." He went on as if she hadn't spoken. "He saw me. He struggled toward me. The tears were on his face, and he kept saying, 'I'm sorry, I'm sorry,' over and over again. 'I didn't mean it. I'm sorry.' He said it the whole time. He kept pulling things off me so he could drag me out. He kept saying it. 'I'm sorry.'"

She didn't know what to say. Was it better or worse for Matt that he remembered more? She didn't know, but she knew that Matt himself was on the verge of tears.

"It's all right." She murmured the words as gently as if she were comforting a child. "It's all right."

He met her gaze then, and his eyes were clouded with tears. "He was just a boy. He looked like a little kid who'd hurt himself. He looked like David."

His face crumbled then, and he reached for her almost blindly. Her arms went around him, and she cradled him close, feeling his labored breathing and the salt tears on his face. Her cheek was against his wounded one, and she stroked his hair and kissed him gently, longing to make everything better, and know-ing she couldn't.

He turned his head, just a little, and then his lips touched hers. His arms tightened around her. He kissed her with a kind of desperate longing that made her gasp, and then grasped her heart and wouldn't let go.

This is where I belong. The thought shocked Matt into awareness. He threw himself back in the chair and stared at Miriam in consternation. What had he done? Had he lost his head entirely?

"S-sorry," he stammered. He knew his face must be barn-red. "I didn't mean… I mean…"

He'd better shut up, because he wasn't making any sense. And Miriam was staring at him with her eyes so wide and dazed it was as if she didn't know where she was.

He released the brake and shoved the wheelchair back away from her. He cleared his throat. And his mind still couldn't fathom what had just happened.

He'd kissed her, and somehow he had to make that right. Miriam was a friend, a neighbor, someone who'd helped him immensely and done her best for him. He might have wrecked all that with one careless action.

No, not careless. There'd been nothing careless about it. He'd needed someone. Miriam had been there, helping, as she always was. If she…if they…if there could be anything more between them…

Miriam rose, turning away from him as if she couldn't look at him. Pain shot through him at the hurt he must have caused her. What was she thinking?

Marriage? They weren't teenagers. He couldn't kiss her casually. Not that it had been casual.

No, she wouldn't think he meant marriage. She was

more sensible than that. He couldn't marry. He had nothing to offer anyone now, and Miriam knew it.

He had to say something. "Miriam, I... I didn't mean that to happen. You've been so good to me...to the whole family. I don't want to mess this up."

There. That at least sounded as if he had a brain in his head.

With her back still to him, Miriam straightened. She turned toward him slowly, and her face was composed now. "It's all right." Her voice trembled, and then steadied. "I know you didn't mean anything. Forget it, and I will, too."

Despite her words and her expression, Matt knew that things were not all right. Her hands clasped each other so tightly that her knuckles were strained and white. But what else could he say?

"Denke," he murmured.

She walked a few steps away from him, fiddling with the exercise bands as if she needed something to occupy her hands. She shook her head, and then she spoke.

"Do you think you'll need to do something about what you remembered?"

If her voice quivered a little, he guessed it was only natural under the circumstances. The line of thoughts opened up by her question had him feeling shaky, as well.

"I hadn't thought of it that way." He tried to find his way through the confusion in his mind. "Do you mean tell that lawyer?"

"Yah. Maybe...maybe it would make a difference

in the trial. I mean, if they knew that the driver tried to help you."

"Yah, yah, you're right. And the others…" He gestured toward the rest of the house. Then he shook his head. "I don't think I can go through it again right now."

"I understand." Miriam's voice was gentle.

His gaze was drawn to her face. "Could you…could you find Daad and tell him the gist of it? So maybe he can help me figure out how to handle it? I know it's not fair to ask you…"

She broke in before he finished. "For sure. I'll go and find him now."

Judging by the speed at which she hurried to the door, he guessed that she was eager to get away from him, at least for the moment. He couldn't blame her, because he felt that way himself. He had to think… about her, about what was going to happen, about what she meant to him.

By the time Miriam reached home that afternoon, she felt as if she'd run miles and climbed several mountains. Had she done the best she could to help Matt's family deal with the upcoming trial? And, just as important to her, what was she going to do about Matt? About the fact that Matt kissed her, combined with her love for him and his…what? Friendship? Reliance? What was it he felt for her, or did he even know?

Mammi was in the kitchen, as usual. She took one look at Miriam and reached for the refrigerator door.

"You look as if you're about to drop from the heat.

Sit down. I've got some iced tea all ready for you. And there's a fresh batch of oatmeal cookies on the cooling rack."

Miriam veered toward the counter to grab a couple of cookies and then sank down on her chair. Mammi set a tall glass in front of her, then fetched one for herself and returned to the table.

"There, is that better?" she asked after Miriam had taken a long drink. "You look like you needed it."

"I did." She held the cold glass against her forehead. "Today that lawyer came to talk to Matt. It was upsetting to everyone."

"Including you." Mammi patted her hand. "I can see that, too."

She nodded. "The lawyer insisted that Matt go over everything he remembered from the accident. It was clearly hard on Matt to relive it. I wanted so much to make the man stop."

"I suppose I haven't thought about that part of it." Mammi frowned, considering. "We say justice should roll down, but what if the justice causes more harm to someone who's been hurt already?"

"That's just what I felt. And then he assumed Matt would go into court and tell it all again. He acted like it was all routine." She caught back several angry things she'd like to say.

"He was very young, and I guess he was just doing his job. Matt said no. He'd done what he should, but he wouldn't go and testify against the driver." Tears stung her eyes at the thought. "He forgave him. He thought he never could, but he did."

"Ach, I'm wonderful glad." Mamm's fingers tightened on her arm. "If he can forgive, then he's on the way to getting over it."

"It's not easy," she murmured, seeing the pain in Matt's face again. "But it's best for him. For all of them."

She almost went on and told Mammi about the decision Matt and his parents had made, that they would tell the district attorney about how the driver had tried to help. She caught herself just in time. That news wasn't hers to share until they'd done it.

Before Mammi could ask the question that lingered in her eyes, feet thudded on the porch, and the three youngest boys barreled in. They were wet and muddy—they'd obviously been cooling off in the creek.

"Ach, what have I told you!" Mammi jumped up, scolding. "Go back out right now and wash off before you come tracking mud into my kitchen. Go on." She made a shooing motion, but then she grabbed Sammy before he could leave and turned him around to face her.

"What is this?" She touched his face, where a red bump was swelling as they watched. "Another person with a black eye in this house? How did you get this?"

Sammy wiggled, trying to get away from her hand. "Just a bump. It's nothing."

The twins exchanged glances and began backing out the screen door. Without seeming to look at them, Mammi responded.

"You two stay right here."

"But Mammi, our dirty feet—" John Thomas had a righteous tone that didn't fool anyone.

"What do you know about this?" She fixed them with a maternal frown.

"Nothing," John Thomas said glibly.

James wasn't so accomplished. He blushed, stubbed his toe into the floor, and murmured, "It wasn't our fault."

"All right, I'll tell it," Sammy said. "You two would mess it up." He turned to Mammi, with a side look at Miriam that seemed full of a warning she didn't understand.

"Some of the guys came over to get in the creek with us. And one…"

"Out with it. Who, and what did he do? Have you been fighting?"

"Not exactly fighting." He grinned. "I just ducked him to make him take back what he said. And he hit my eye with his elbow by accident."

"Who?" she repeated, implacable.

"Jimmy Frey," he said reluctantly.

Miriam blinked, suddenly right in the middle of it. Jimmy was Nola Frey's boy.

"What did he say?" Mammi was firm about knowing it all.

"It was something about me, wasn't it?" In that moment, Miriam realized how foolish her worries about what had happened in Ohio were compared to real problems. "It's okay. Tell us."

"It was dumb. He said he heard that Miriam got into trouble because of some guy while she was out in Ohio. And I said she did not. And he said it again, so I ducked him in the creek. And I'm not sorry," he added defiantly.

Miriam had never realized how hard it must be to convince a boy of the value of nonviolence. She wanted to laugh, but Mammi wouldn't appreciate it.

"Listen, it's okay." She went to put her hands on Sammy's shoulders, realizing how tall he'd gotten in recent months. "He's just got it all mixed up. There was a boy I was helping when he was sick, and he just acted silly. He got a crush on me. That's all it was." She hesitated. That was all a ten-year-old needed to know, anyway. "You understand what a crush is?"

Sammy considered. "You mean like when I took all those flowers to Teacher Gloria when she took over our classes that time?"

Mammi gave an odd sound that might have been a cough or a laugh.

"Yah, just like that. So you don't need to duck Jimmy in the creek anymore. But you can tell him the truth…that the boy had a crush on me, but I didn't do anything wrong."

"I knew you didn't do anything wrong," he told her loudly. "And if he says that again—"

"Well, he won't say that again, will he, once he knows the truth?"

"I guess not. But I would, if he did."

Miriam decided not to take that on. "Go on out and get washed, the lot of you."

Mammi nodded. "Go."

The door slammed behind them, and Miriam was

unable to restrain the laughter. "Poor Jimmy. And it's all so foolish. You and Daad were right all along. I didn't do anything wrong, and I shouldn't have tried to hide it."

Mammi put her arm around Miriam in a tight hug. "Yah. But it's not nice to have people gossiping like that, and I'll be setting Nola Frey right just as soon as I can."

"You don't need to."

"I do." She seemed to look forward to it. "Was it just Sammy that made you see?"

"Not just that." She shook her head. "I was self-centered, thinking so much about the fact that I had been humiliated. It was foolish in comparison to what other people have to fret about. I'm ashamed of myself."

She wouldn't be thinking about it any longer, she knew. That was one thing learned from this time with the King family. And if she had to leave her job only half-done because of what she felt for Matt, well, she'd do it. She could have a satisfying life without marriage, even if she didn't see how right now.

Chapter Fourteen

Matt had plenty of things to fill his mind, but he'd tossed and turned through the night, thinking about Miriam. And he still hadn't come to any conclusions.

Was it even possible to make things right with Miriam? She'd said she'd forget about that kiss, but he suspected she couldn't. If they'd both been teenagers, a casual kiss wouldn't be out of line. But at their age, it meant something far more serious.

He'd punched his pillow a few times during the night each time he came to that conclusion. The pillow had survived it, but he hadn't found any answers.

Fortunately the family had been occupied during breakfast by the revelation of what had happened between him and the driver of the car. Mammi was obviously relieved. She hated to think ill of anyone, no matter what they'd done, and his revelation of the boy's attitude and his efforts to help had dissolved whatever barrier was left in her to forgiveness.

It wouldn't be right to say she was happy. She was

still grieving for David and probably always would be. But there was a peace about her that he almost envied.

He was far from being at peace, at least with himself. He glanced at the clock as Mammi and Betsy finished the breakfast dishes. Miriam would be here soon, if she were coming. But would she?

"I believe I'll go out on the porch to wait for Miriam." He pushed his chair to the door, and Betsy came hurrying to help him.

"You'll like it," she told him. "The air is nice and clear today."

"Like fall?" He rolled onto the porch.

She shrugged. "Maybe. The kids will be going back to school soon." For an instant Betsy looked as if she wasn't sure what that meant for her. She'd finished her schooling in the spring, and he realized he'd no idea what she wanted to do next.

"What about you?"

She shrugged. "I was thinking about asking to be a helper at school, but maybe…well, maybe I'm needed here more."

"Because of me." He didn't really have to ask why. Her life had been changed, too, he reminded himself. But maybe that plan, at least, could be saved.

He caught her hand and squeezed it. "I think you ought to go ahead and try for a job at school. Look at me—I'm doing better every day. And you'd be a good teacher's aide."

"Do you think so?" Her face brightened in an instant.

"Yah, I think so." He patted her hand. "Go after what you want, okay?"

She hesitated and then nodded. "I guess maybe I will." She skipped back inside, all smiles.

You're spreading cheer all over the place, he told himself wryly. Now what about trying to make things better with Miriam?

He turned the chair, looking toward the path by which Miriam came. Maybe he should make sure she understood he couldn't marry anybody. That might ease things between them if she had any feelings for him. Or would she find it insulting? He suspected he didn't know as much about women as he'd thought he did.

He'd probably been foolish enough to think he did because of his popularity with girls like Liva Ann. But Miriam was a completely different person from Liva Ann—a grown-up, with a mind and a determination and a full heart to share.

Matt was still trying to figure out what to do when he caught sight of Miriam's slender figure moving toward him along the path that bordered the field. He watched, aware of a funny disturbance in his heart, almost as if it tried to tell him something.

Shoving the thought away, he wheeled himself down the ramp so he could meet her at the driveway. The trouble was that the closer she came, the stronger the feeling grew, and the less able he was to deal with it.

He was almost relieved when she was close enough to talk to so that he was forced to make a decision. Pretend that nothing had happened and carry on as usual?

He knew suddenly that he couldn't. It wasn't fair to Miriam to pretend he hadn't kissed her. It wasn't fair to himself, either. If he had feelings for her, the best thing was to confront them.

Miriam came up to him, her smile strained. "Are we going somewhere before we start on your exercises?"

"Not exactly. I think maybe we should talk a bit first."

"If this is about what happened yesterday, I'd rather not," she said quickly, actually taking a step back.

That decided him. They couldn't go on like this, no matter what.

"We have to. Please, Miriam." He gestured toward the seat under the apple tree. "Let's go over to the bench and talk. No one will bother us."

She stiffened, as if she would refuse to move, but then she nodded. Seizing the back of the chair, she helped him maneuver it across the lawn to the bench in the shade.

At his gesture, she sat down and looked at him, her eyes wary.

He drew the chair over so that he faced her—knee to knee, the way they'd been during those moments when he'd lost control of himself.

After taking a deep breath, he plunged in. "I know you said we'd just forget about what happened between us, but we can't. Or anyway, I can't. I didn't plan it, but it happened."

"I know that," she said in a rush. "Please, Matt, can't we just get back to work on your exercises? I don't want to ruin that by mixing up personal feelings in it. You're doing so well."

He shook his head, feeling the need to explain…

to apologize… He wasn't sure what, but he knew he couldn't pretend it never happened.

"Look, I… I can't deny that I have feelings for you. You've…well, you've brought me back to living again. But I can't offer you anything."

He was doing this badly, saying all the wrong things. He should have stuck a bandage over his mouth. But at least her expression had softened a little.

She leaned forward, touching his hand gently. "I'm not asking you for anything, Matt. I want to help you. Any other feelings I have…" she stumbled over the words "…well, that doesn't affect my work. I won't let it."

Other feelings. He repeated the words silently.

"I just want to be sure you understand." He drew in a breath and fought for the words. "Whatever I feel, I know that marriage isn't for me. I can't support a wife, I don't have anything to offer, and I won't take pity."

Miriam sat rigid for a long moment, staring at Matt. His words had been bombarding her heart, with every word seeming to add another blow.

But this…this was the last straw. The only thing she could do was either break into a storm of weeping or explode in a display of temper. And she wasn't going to cry in front of him.

She shot to her feet. "What do you mean? I haven't asked you to marry me. And you certain sure haven't asked me."

"Look, I…"

"And if I did want to marry you, it would be because I love you." She swept on, carried by a wave of feeling too strong to be denied. "That's the only reason I'd marry anybody. As far as I'm concerned, loving doesn't have anything to do with what somebody has to offer or whether that person has a beautiful face or two good legs. It has to do with loving the whole person, the way they are inside. That's what I—"

She stopped, knowing she was on the verge of telling him she loved him. Still, if he didn't realize it by now, he wasn't paying attention. She'd left him speechless, and she couldn't go on much longer. Soon they'd just sit and stare, like two statues.

"I'm going home," she announced. "I'm taking the day off. If you want me to come back to work tomorrow…well, just let me know."

No more…she couldn't handle any more. Miriam wanted to run, but she wouldn't let herself. Walking away, she was shaking inside, but her legs kept on moving. She could only hope that she could get to the haven of her room before her family asked her questions.

Matt figured he couldn't have made any more of a mess of that conversation if he'd intended to. Somehow he'd said all the wrong things. He'd just wanted to give both of them room to pull back, but he'd managed to hurt Miriam and chase her away.

After struggling to turn the chair in the grass, Matt finally got it done and moving, which was an accomplishment if he'd felt like celebrating. He tried to spot Miriam, but she'd already vanished around the curve in the path.

By the time he was nearing the ramp, Betsy had spotted him, and she came running to help. With her assistance, he reached the porch, where he stopped.

"Is Mammi here?"

"No. Don't you remember? She was going to help at the cleanup day at the schoolhouse. Do you need her?"

He shook his head. What he wanted was to avoid any questions, so it was just as well she'd gone out. But there was still Betsy to deal with, and he felt sure she'd have something to say.

"Where's Miriam? Why did she leave you out here by yourself?" She studied his face. "You hurt her feelings, didn't you?"

Annoyed, he frowned at her. "You're getting awful sassy, you know that?"

"I'm growing up, you mean. Well, what did you do?" She put her hand on the arm of the chair as if to keep him from getting away before he'd answered.

"Nothing." Neither of them believed that. "I didn't mean to do anything. I was just explaining why I figured I wouldn't get married. I mean, that's out of the question."

"Why?" Betsy didn't let go. "I mean, why couldn't you get married? You were going to marry Liva Ann, weren't you?"

He shuddered at the thought of how unhappy they'd have made each other. "No," he said firmly. "Anyway, that doesn't matter. Just let me get to my room."

Betsy stepped back and then went and opened the door for him. "I still say you hurt her feelings. After all, she loves you."

"She… What makes you think that?" He turned his face away, not wanting her to read his expression. "Did she say so?"

"She didn't need to say so," Betsy said scornfully. "Me and Mammi both saw it over a week ago. And we thought it would be a good thing."

How much else, he wondered, had he missed about what went on behind his back?

"Listen, Betsy, be serious."

"I *am* serious," she protested. "Ask Mammi if you don't believe me. Miriam loves you, and you ought to ask her to marry you. There's room for both of you here, right?"

"I can't," he said automatically.

"Well, why not? Miriam doesn't care about that scar, ain't so? She's not like Liva Ann. And you love her, don't you?"

The question hit him like something exploding over his head. Was that what was the matter with him? Did he love her?

The answer filled his heart. He loved her. It had been her all along, and he hadn't seen it.

Panic swamped him. If he'd lost her—

He grabbed Betsy's arm. "Where's Daad and Josh?"

"They went to the lumberyard, and then they're going to stop at the school. Why? What do you need? I can do it."

"Looks like you'll have to." He thought quickly. Sending a message wouldn't help. He had to get over there and find Miriam before it was too late.

The buggy? No, he wouldn't be able to get up into it without Daad to help. But the pony cart…

"Can you get the pony cart out and harness Dolly? Quickly?"

"Yah, sure I can. Why? Where am I going?"

"Not you. Or at least not alone. Me. I have to get over to see Miriam right now."

Betsy looked at him, understanding growing on her face. Breaking into a huge grin, she whirled and sped toward the barn, moving so fast it was as if she hardly touched the ground.

He took the wheelchair back down to the road. He'd have gone to get the pony himself, but if the wheelchair scared Dolly, they'd be that much longer getting there.

So he waited with what patience he could muster, hands clenched. He should have been thinking about how he would get into the pony cart, but his thoughts were completely revolving around Miriam.

There was no real need to rush, he told himself, but he didn't believe it. He had to get to her, to tell her. This time get it right. This time tell her that he loved her.

It seemed forever before Betsy came back driving the pony cart, but it couldn't have been more than a few minutes. She set the brake, climbed out, and ran around the cart to help him.

"What's the best way to do this?" She grabbed his arm as if planning to pull him into the cart by sheer force.

"Slowly." He mentally measured the distance up to the cart seat. He could do it. He had to. "It's a good thing I put the brace on my leg this morning," he said.

"Just get me as close as possible to the seat, but facing forward."

She wiggled the chair into position and stopped when he told her. "What are you going to do now?"

"Help me stand, first. Then, when I'm in position, I want you to go round and get in the other side. You put your arms around my chest and pull me toward the seat while I push myself up."

Betsy hesitated. "You sure you're not going to get hurt? Daadi would kill me if I let you get hurt."

"He wouldn't. Just remember that if you don't help, I'll do it myself."

That convinced her. Using the side of the cart with one hand and the arm of the wheelchair with the other, he managed to get to his feet with her help.

"Now hold on tight while I get on the other side." Betsy patted his arm and scurried around the cart.

He was concentrating too hard to speak. He'd stay upright. He had to. He was backed against the cart, feeling the seat with one hand, when Betsy clambered in. In a moment, her strong young arms circled his chest.

"Okay," she said, once satisfied with her position. "Are you ready?"

"Ready." Hands braced, he used his better leg to push against the cart wheel, levering himself up and over while pulling with his hands. Betsy, breathing hard, pulled him too, bumping his back against the side bar.

He seemed to be balanced in midair for a moment, pushing and straining, the sweat pouring off him. Then

Betsy gave a huge pull, he shoved as hard as possible, and he dragged himself onto the seat, sprawling across it.

"Good girl, Dolly," he breathed. "She didn't move an inch. And good for you." He clasped Betsy in a one-armed hug, busy holding on with the other. "Just pull my legs in or they'll be dragging on the ground."

By the time she'd done that, he was sitting up. The pony cart, with its memories of dozens, maybe hundreds of trips, seemed to welcome him. He reached for the reins, but Betsy beat him to it.

"No way. You've done enough for one day. What Miriam is going to say, I can't even guess." She slapped the lines, and Dolly moved off. The pony cart bounced over every little bump in the drive on the way to the road and Miriam.

Matt held on tight. He didn't have to guess about what he wanted Miriam to say. He wanted her to say yes.

Chapter Fifteen

By the time she'd reached the privacy of her room, Miriam discovered that the urge to cry had left her. Something about walking all the way home had drained it away, leaving her...empty. That was the only word she could think of that fit.

She wanted to be angry with Matt, because that would be easier. She knew exactly what he was thinking. He didn't want people to see him this way. He'd pushed away all the progress he made, convincing himself that he wasn't whole enough to gain a woman's love.

He already had it. Didn't he realize that? They could build a life together—a good life that included his family and her family and the farm...

But not if he didn't love her. Not if he didn't believe she could love him.

Trying to distract herself, she walked to the bed and slumped down on it. She should find something to do with herself. Mammi had gone to the workday at the school, of course, and Daad and the boys were out about the farm. They probably didn't even realize she'd come back. But they would, and she'd have to explain herself.

Miriam pressed her fingers to her temples, feeling the pounding of an oncoming headache, no doubt from suppressing her tears.

She stared at the hooked rug Grossmammi had made for her bedroom, all deep rose and soft green. It had been an act of love, and just pressing her feet against it brought her grandmother's love flowing around her like a hug.

How long she sat there, she didn't know, but eventually she heard a sound out in the driveway—voices. Before she could go and look, feet came pounding up the steps. Was someone hurt?

She hurried to the door in time to catch the twins. "What are you doing? Is something wrong?"

John Thomas grabbed one hand, and James the other, and they tugged.

"You have to come. Right now!" John Thomas was so excited he was nearly jumping. "Hurry!"

"Yah, hurry," James added. "Matt is here. He wants to see you."

"Matt? He can't be. How would he get here? If this is a joke—"

"No joke. He's here, and he wants you." Her brothers dragged her forward, with John Thomas being the spokesman, as usual. "Now, now, now!"

Her heart thudding with a mixture of fear and excitement, she rushed down the steps, the boys getting in her way and nearly sending her headlong. They raced ahead of her across the kitchen and out, slamming the screen door, but she wasn't far behind them.

She shot outside and then stopped, unable to believe what she was seeing. The pony cart stood in the driveway, with Dolly cropping peacefully at the grass along the edge. Impossibly, Matthew sat in the cart, his gaze fixed on her.

"Aren't you going to say anything?" he asked, his voice gentle. There was something in his eyes that she hadn't seen before…something that set her heart pounding so loudly, she could hear it.

"I… I don't know what to say." She moved to the pony cart, brushing Betsy and the twins out of her way. "How? What?" She gestured helplessly.

It was Matt, the old Matt—sure of himself, cheerful—who smiled at her. "Come up here and I'll tell you all about it." He held out his hand to her. "Because if I get down, I'll never get back up again."

Could he actually be laughing at himself, the way he used to? She reached for his hand and felt him pull her into the cart.

Matt looked at her, started to speak, and then stopped. "Betsy," he said loudly, "there's too many people around here."

Betsy giggled, then grabbed a twin by each hand. "Come on, guys. Show me the chickens, okay?" She led them away despite John Thomas's loud objections.

Then they were alone, sitting close together, and she couldn't think of a single thing to say. She stared down at her hands, clasping themselves in her lap as if independent of her.

"Wouldn't you look at me, Miriam?" His voice was low, just for her. "I can't tell you I love you unless you do."

Her gaze leaped to his before she could think about it. "You... What did you say?"

"You heard. It's what I should have said before. I love you." He put his hands over hers, and his touch immediately stopped their straining. "I didn't even realize it, and it was there all along." He touched her cheek, running his finger lightly along the curve to her lips.

Her breath stopped, and all she could do was look at him with her heart showing plainly in her face. "Are you sure?" she murmured.

"Very sure."

His head bent, and his lips closed on hers, warm and confident and loving. The world seemed to spin around them and then draw slowly away, leaving them locked in each other's arms as if they were the only people in the universe.

Miriam could hear his heart beating, sure and steady. She sensed the feelings flowing back and forth between them...love, passion, longing, friendship, caring. She had known she loved him, but she'd never imagined it would be like this.

Slowly he pulled back far enough to look at her. "Now that we have that settled, will you marry me? I don't know what we'll live on or how well I can hope to be, but I know I want the future, whatever it is, to be with you."

She caressed his scarred cheek. "Yah, I'll marry you. In fact, if you hadn't asked me, I might have had to ask you."

He chuckled, his voice low and his arms tightening. "I'd like to hear that."

"And I know just how we'll live, no matter how well you become. We'll live on the farm, and we'll share our families. With Josh's help, one day you'll be running the farm yourself."

"You're sure of that?"

"I'm sure." She traced the line of his smile. Smiles had been scarce for a time, but now it was her job to be sure he smiled often. "One day we'll have sons to help you work the farm...maybe one of them named David, if you want."

He nodded, his eyes shining. "Mammi and Daad would like that. But how about a girl?"

"Yah, there has to be a girl," she said lightly, loving the way he sounded when he laughed at her, and the way his voice rumbled in his chest so she could feel it. "My mother and your mother will demand it, don't you think?"

"They will." He caught her hand and brought it to his lips for a kiss. "Ach, Miriam, life doesn't always turn out the way you expect it to. Are you sure you're willing to take a chance on me?"

"I'm sure," she said, feeling it with every heartbeat, every breath. "Whatever comes, we'll deal with it together, with God's help."

His smile was very sweet. "Yah. We will." It sounded like a promise.

She glanced over his shoulder. "Here come the twins, and your sister, and my daad, and my other brothers. I think you'll have to be ready to take them all on as part of your family."

"That sounds like a great idea." He followed the direction of her gaze, smiling.

She watched as they reached the pony cart. Daad didn't seem to need any explanations. One look at their flushed faces must have been enough. He reached out and grasped Matt's hand, smiling, while the boys climbed in the back of the pony cart, eager to be part of whatever happened.

Two families would become one—one noisy, funny, sad, troublesome, loving family, with God in control. She couldn't think of anything better.

* * * * *

If you enjoyed this story,
don't miss the previous books in the
Brides of Lost Creek series from Marta Perry:

Find more great reads at www.LoveInspired.com

Dear Reader,

Thank you for coming back to visit Lost Creek once more. It's one of my favorite places, and I hope you enjoy yourself. This time, the third of the three cousins has her opportunity to find the unique gift God has given her to serve others, but also to find true love.

I really like Miriam, with her gentle touch and her firm manner when it comes to recalcitrant patients. She spends her life giving to others, but she hadn't yet taken the time to let others give to her. She reminds me of so many people I know who are first in line when it comes to giving help, but reluctant to admit that they need help themselves. Sometimes, like Miriam, they find God's blessing in both receiving and giving.

I hope you'll let me know if you enjoy my story. You can find me on the web at www.martaperry.com or on Facebook at www.facebook.com/MartaPerrybooks, or you can email me at mpjohn@ptd.net.

Blessings,

Marta Perry

COMING NEXT MONTH FROM
Love Inspired

THEIR SECRET COURTSHIP
by Emma Miller

Resisting pressure from her mother to marry, Bay Stutzman is determined to keep her life exactly as it is. Until Mennonite David Jansen accidentally runs her wagon off the road. Now Bay must decide whether sharing a life with David is worth leaving behind everything she's ever known...

CARING FOR HER AMISH FAMILY
The Amish of New Hope • by Carrie Lighte

Forced to move into a dilapidated old house when entrusted with caring for her *Englisch* nephew, Amish apron maker Anke Bachman must turn to newcomer Josiah Mast for help with repairs. Afraid of being judged by his new community, Josiah tries to distance himself from the pair but can't stop his feelings from blossoming...

FINDING HER WAY BACK
K-9 Companions • by Lisa Carter

After a tragic event leaves widower Detective Rob Melbourne injured and his little girl emotionally scarred, he enlists the services of therapy dog handler Juliet Newkirk and her dog, Moose. But will working with the woman he once loved prove to be a distraction for Rob...or the second chance his family needs?

THE REBEL'S RETURN
The Ranchers of Gabriel Bend • by Myra Johnson

When a family injury calls him home to Gabriel Bend, Samuel Navarro shocks everyone by arriving with a baby in tow. His childhood love, Joella James, reluctantly agrees to babysit his infant daughter. But can she forget their tangled past and discover a future with this newly devoted father?

AN ORPHAN'S HOPE
by Christina Miller

Twice left at the altar, preacher Jase Armstrong avoids commitment at all costs—until he inherits his cousin's three-day-old baby. Pushing him further out of his comfort zone is nurse Erin Tucker and her lessons on caring for an infant. But can Erin convince him he's worthy of being a father *and* a husband?

HER SMALL-TOWN REFUGE
by Jennifer Slattery

Seeking a fresh start, Stephanie Thornton and her daughter head to Sage Creek. But when the veterinary clinic where she works is robbed, all evidence points to Stephanie. Proving her innocence to her boss, Caden Stoughton, might lead to the new life she's been searching for...

LOOK FOR THESE AND OTHER LOVE INSPIRED BOOKS WHEREVER BOOKS ARE SOLD, INCLUDING MOST BOOKSTORES, SUPERMARKETS, DISCOUNT STORES AND DRUGSTORES.

LICNM0122A

Get 4 FREE REWARDS!

We'll send you 2 FREE Books plus 2 FREE Mystery Gifts.

Love Inspired books feature uplifting stories where faith helps guide you through life's challenges and discover the promise of a new beginning.

FREE Value Over $20

YES! Please send me 2 FREE Love Inspired Romance novels and my 2 FREE mystery gifts (gifts are worth about $10 retail). After receiving them, if I don't wish to receive any more books, I can return the shipping statement marked "cancel." If I don't cancel, I will receive 6 brand-new novels every month and be billed just $5.24 each for the regular-print edition or $5.99 each for the larger-print edition in the U.S., or $5.74 each for the regular-print edition or $6.24 each for the larger-print edition in Canada. That's a savings of at least 13% off the cover price. It's quite a bargain! Shipping and handling is just 50¢ per book in the U.S. and $1.25 per book in Canada.* I understand that accepting the 2 free books and gifts places me under no obligation to buy anything. I can always return a shipment and cancel at any time. The free books and gifts are mine to keep no matter what I decide.

Choose one: ☐ **Love Inspired Romance**
Regular-Print
(105/305 IDN GNWC)

☐ **Love Inspired Romance**
Larger-Print
(122/322 IDN GNWC)

Name (please print)

Address   Apt. #

City   State/Province   Zip/Postal Code

Email: Please check this box ☐ if you would like to receive newsletters and promotional emails from Harlequin Enterprises ULC and its affiliates. You can unsubscribe anytime.

Mail to the **Harlequin Reader Service:**
IN U.S.A.: P.O. Box 1341, Buffalo, NY 14240-8531
IN CANADA: P.O. Box 603, Fort Erie, Ontario L2A 5X3

Want to try 2 free books from another series? Call 1-800-873-8635 or visit www.ReaderService.com.